USA *Today* Bestselling Author

Dale Mayer

MAN
DOWN
MASTERS

MASTERS: MAN DOWN, BOOK 2
Beverly Dale Mayer
Valley Publishing Ltd.

ISBN-13: 978-1-778863-26-4
Print Edition

Books in This Series:

Jasper, Book 1

Masters, Book 2

Gideon, Book 3

Tristan, Book 4

About This Book

There is no greater motive than bloodlust, DNA, and revenge mixed up in a cocktail of hatred …

Masters has joined Jasper's investigation team, when they realize another investigator went missing four months ago, yet his case is on hold. Part of the issue is that Masters needs to figure out who on the existing team is trustworthy. He reaches out to the missing investigator's sister, looking for answers.

Elizabeth has been seeking answers over her brother's disappearance ever since the last time she spoke to him. With no leads, no tips, and no sign of him, the case ran cold. To her, it seemed no one cared. Having Masters show up at her door, asking questions all over again, sparks anger and hope in her.

Maybe this time they can find out what happened to the only family Elizabeth has left …

Sign up to be notified of all Dale's releases here!
https://geni.us/DaleNews

PROLOGUE

MASTERS WOODROW ENTERED the building where the investigators worked, which was dark. Turning on the lights, he headed to the small area that Jasper had used as an office. Sitting down and using his log-in credentials, Masters started the research he needed to do. When he heard a noise, he looked up to see Sam glaring at him. Masters stared back at him. "You got a problem? You take it up with Jasper." Then he returned to his research.

"It's Jasper who I've got a problem with," he barked.

Masters shrugged, refusing to face Sam. "Then take it up with the brass. Not my problem."

"Seriously, you're on this team now too?"

"I am," he declared.

"What about Jasper?"

"Jasper is too. He's getting some much-needed rest right now. In case you didn't hear about the mess happening today, he's been busy."

Sam shrugged. "It wasn't all that bad."

"If that's what you think, you don't have all the details." Masters stopped, looked up at him, and intensely studied the man for the first time. Sam looked to be about late forties, a hothead by the sound of it, and a little bit gone to pot. He had a good-size middle rim of flab all the way around his belly, just above his belt loops. His coloring was pale, a little bit blotchy, and his hair was thinning on top already. "What's your problem with Jasper anyway?"

"He walked in here like he was the boss and took over. He already knew Morgan's the boss."

"Morgan was an *acting* boss," Masters clarified, narrowing his gaze at Sam. "How come you didn't tell your bosses how you felt?"

Sam shifted uneasily and scoffed. "You're just like him, aren't you? You're probably friends. Is that how you got the job?"

"I don't have to do things like that," he replied. "My reputation precedes me, as does Jasper's, as does Mason's. This is what I do. I was coming in to take a job on this base as it was, yet in a slightly different position. However, after seeing Mason shot down right in front of me, you can bet I wanted in on it."

"Oh, yeah, shot in front of you, but you didn't do anything to stop it, did you?"

"It would be a little hard to stop a sniper plan set up days, if not months in advance," he stated. He noted Sam stood unsteadily in front of him. "Are you drunk?"

"No, I'm not drunk," he snapped. "What are you doing here at this hour of the night?"

"What are *you* doing here at this hour of the night, drunk or not?" Not liking anything about him, Masters added, "Either you need to get the hell out of here or sit down and do some work. I am working myself. So you choose what you're doing, but make a decision now."

"And if I don't?" Sam asked, his hands in his pockets, but, sure enough, he remained unsteady on his feet.

Masters got up, walked closer, and smelled the alcohol. "You get your drunk ass out of here," he ordered. "Leave your key card behind, and do not come in until you contact me and I've met you outside of work somewhere long enough to confirm that you're sober."

"What are you gonna—"

"And, if I find out that you're not sober and that you can't stay sober for forty-eight hours straight, you'll be under drug testing and suspended from work," Masters declared calmly, as he turned Sam around and gave him a shove toward the exit door.

Protesting the whole way, Sam started to slur his words to the point that Masters was worried he would have to pick him up to toss him out.

When he got him outside the building, a couple other guys were hanging around, loudly laughing and talking and drinking. "Are you with them?"

"So what if I am?"

"That's fine, but, in the meantime, you are not allowed to drive tonight either."

"You can't stop me," Sam bellowed.

But Masters braced him, quickly shoving him against the wall, taking his car keys and his office key card. "Now get yourself home."

"How the hell am I supposed to do that? You just took my wheels."

"I did, and I'll take even more the longer you stand here. Now get lost," he snapped. Then he watched as Sam stumbled away.

Shaking his head, Masters returned to the office and quickly sent Jasper a text. Masters wasn't sure what the hell was going on, but how the hell did that guy Sam keep his job here? Maybe they did need a couple new people on this investigation team. He sent a quick text to Morgan, asking him about Sam's condition as well.

When the phone rang, Morgan was on the other end. "What the hell are you doing there?"

"I'm here because Jasper is at home after an incident tonight," he explained. "I'm working on Mason's case. Found Sam in the office, stumbling drunk."

Silence came on the other end. "Oh, damn."

"Meaning?"

"Meaning, he fell off the stupid wagon again."

"And how much of a problem is that?"

"It shouldn't be a problem at all."

"I just took his car keys off him and his access card." He picked up the card and frowned. "Except for one thing."

"What's that?" Morgan asked.

"The key card that I took off Sam doesn't have his name on it."

"What do you mean?"

"The key I have in my hand, which I just took off Sam, has a different name on it. … Nicholas."

"Nicholas, Nicholas Woodrow?" Morgan asked.

Masters frowned at the last name. He had no relative that he knew of by the name of Nicholas. Yet easier to remember the guy's name, for sure. Masters twisted the key card in the light to see it better, noting the tone change in Morgan's reply. "Yes, Nicholas Woodrow. Why? You know him?"

"Yeah, he disappeared from our department and the base about four months ago," he shared. "He was involved in another case on Coronado base."

"What do you mean, *another case?*"

"Nicholas was working another shooting."

CHAPTER 1

NOT TOO MANY hours later, Masters returned to the department and headed straight back to Jasper's office. As soon as he got inside, he shut the door, then sat down and sent Jasper a text. **Good morning. I'm at your desk and need permission to access your system again.** His phone rang almost immediately.

"You're in there now, *huh?*"

"Yes, I signed off when I left late last night—well early this morning actually—so I'll need you to get me logged in again, as well as permission to be here."

"Done and done," Jasper stated. "What are you after so bright and early after working late?"

"I'm after any information that we can find on this Nicholas guy."

"What's that about?" he asked curiously.

Masters half smiled and replied, "I wondered if you knew anything about it."

"No. I don't. Fill me in."

Masters quickly shared the little bit he knew. "That's what I got from Morgan, though it seems as if there ought to be more than that."

"Maybe he just didn't choose to share," Jasper replied.

"That's what I was wondering," he noted, "so I wanted to cut the circuitous route in half and get the information myself." He listened as Jasper gave him the log-in information for the day, and Masters quickly had access to the computer system again. He added, "And you need to clear it with whomever because I'm pretty sure we've got an all-out fight coming up."

"Probably," Jasper agreed. "Yet, with any luck, not so much. I'll be there soon."

"You sure you're ready to come back in?" Masters asked, a note of humor in his tone.

"Just because I might want to stay out doesn't mean it's a good idea."

"No, of course not. I'll see you when you get here." Then Masters quickly hung up.

He didn't know how long it would take before the rest of the team realized he was in here. He'd walked in fairly easily, and nobody had questioned his presence, but he knew that wouldn't last. He'd hoped that he would make it until Jasper arrived, but, when the door opened about thirty minutes later, he looked up to see Sam glaring at him, Morgan at his side.

"You have no right to be here," Sam declared. "You were way out of line last night."

A man behind them spoke up and said, "Hold up a minute. Don't start without me."

Masters looked up with relief to see Jasper striding toward them.

"I okayed it."

"You have no right to okay anything," Sam snapped.

Something was just so wrong with Sam's attitude that Masters couldn't believe they kept such a liability around.

He had no reason to even think that way, but something was just wrong about a guy so smug and so difficult to deal with.

As it was, Morgan stared at Jasper. "You got clearance for all this?" he asked.

Jasper looked at both and announced, "This is Masters. I've worked with him before. He'll be our secret weapon."

"Like he's some secret weapon or that we even need one." Sam snorted.

Oddly enough, Morgan, who had temporarily been leading this department, nodded. "Might not be a bad idea at that," he murmured. He turned and looked at Masters and held out a hand. "Nice to meet you. Sorry for the trouble you had last night."

Masters shook his hand and nodded. "Likewise."

Sam didn't say anything but turned and stormed out.

Masters looked over at Jasper. "We had quite the chat last night. Not a fan of yours, it seems."

"No, he sure isn't," Jasper confirmed, with a wry look, "but that's okay. He doesn't have to like me, but we do need to clear him."

"It's okay," Morgan noted. "He's been good for the department, and he does good work. He's got an alcohol problem that had been pretty well in hand, after he went through rehab a few years ago. However, it appears he's been struggling recently and fell off the wagon hard last night. He doesn't do well with change, especially when he has no say in it."

"Yet this department is full of changes," Jasper declared.

"It is, indeed, which is another reason why Sam has struggles now," Morgan noted, with a small smile. Looking at Masters, he said, "I don't know what you told him last night, but you scared him sober. If you need anything, let me know." At the doorway, he stopped, looked over at Masters, and added, "I'll put in a request to get your own log-in set up, so you're not coming in under Jasper's."

"Thanks," Masters replied cheerfully, as he watched Morgan leave. Then Masters faced Jasper. "Good timing. That could have gone differently without you here."

"You would have handled it," he said, with a shrug. "Sounds like you handled Sam last night. We'll have to keep a close eye on him, although it explains the reservations I've had about the guy."

"Yeah, drunks lie so much, and the deceit comes off them in waves. Also I highly doubt I'm any secret weapon, by the way."

"You would be surprised. Something is going on here that none of us are getting very clear answers on."

"That's why I want to find out everything there is to know about one Nicholas Woodrow."

"Are you sure it's not just because his last name is the same as yours?" he asked.

Masters shrugged, "Ah, no. Turns out I'm a little deeper than that."

"If you say so," Jasper quipped.

"I do say so," Masters stated in a cool tone. "No relation either, by the way."

"That's good because that's a complication we wouldn't need."

He laughed. "Yeah, that would certainly add another element to the mix, wouldn't it?"

"It would. And not in a good way. So, what have you found out so far?"

"Only that one Nicholas Woodrow was working on an investigation here in this department. I just find it odd that nobody mentioned anything about it, especially considering he just disappeared about four months ago on his way to work one morning. His car was found abandoned on a side road, where the team supposedly found his key card."

Jasper sat down in the chair across from him. "On his way to work?" he asked cautiously.

"He didn't show up, and nobody has seen him since."

"That's not to say that his disappearance was definitely related to an investigation on this base."

Masters nodded. "Right. Last night Morgan told me that the team had been working on another base shooting. Digging in further, I found it was some bar fight gone wrong. So not the connection I expected to link that incident to Mason's shooting. I'm still searching other cases the team dealt with recently. Would be nice if we had access to all their files on the database." Masters raised one eyebrow.

"Yeah. We should have full clearance today. Still, we can't go down that line of thinking without further evidence, but it's a concern that Nicholas never showed up again." Jasper pondered that and added, "Let me bring Morgan back in again." And, with that, he stepped to the door and called out for Morgan.

Morgan appeared a few minutes later, obviously busy, as he was talking on the phone to somebody. He stepped in, ended the phone call, frowned at them, and asked, "What's up?"

"Nicholas Woodrow," Jasper stated.

"Ah." Morgan frowned and nodded. "I was wondering if that was something that needed to be brought up."

"I'm stunned that you didn't think it was something worthy of mention right from the get-go," Jasper declared.

"That's because we haven't had anything to go on. If we thought it was connected somehow, that's a different story."

"Why would you think it couldn't be connected?" Jasper asked, frowning at him.

"All kinds of shit goes on around the base here, and we have a lot of investigations. So absolutely no reason to think that Woodrow's disappearance would have anything to do with the sniper shooting of Mason," Morgan replied. "As far as we know, Nicholas had nothing to do with Mason, and the cases are not connected." He hesitated. "Yet I can see from the look on your face that you don't necessarily agree."

"We don't know that for certain because we didn't know anything about Nicholas's disappearance," Jasper remarked in exasperation. "And it seems foolish to decide that they aren't connected just because you haven't found anything connecting them."

Morgan frowned. "And what other criteria would you use to make that decision?"

"A full investigation of Nicholas gone missing is a start," Jasper pointed out. "Until we do that investigation and clear this up, then we won't know."

"You're free to do that. I've got all the files. It's not in the files I gave you access too already because it involves one of our own, so it was kept in an area with less access, just in case."

"Unlock it now so we can have a look," Jasper said, "and let's see if we can't solve two of these at the same time."

After Morgan did something on his phone, he shared, "Okay, I've given you both access to those files. The thing is, our CO asked us to keep this one under wraps," he added, "so there could be backlash when he finds out I've given you access."

"That's fine," Jasper stated, eyeing him. "If you get called out on it, I'll take the heat."

The look of relief on his face gave Masters some insight into what working here must be like for some of the investigators.

When Morgan left, Masters looked over at Jasper. "We're already checking into the team members, and now we should check out the CO too? Not a good omen."

"Nope, it sure isn't." Jasper groaned. "I sure as hell hope this doesn't involve some BS move up the chain. That's all we need."

"When you say, *BS move*, what do you mean?"

He shrugged. "The usual. I just don't want to find out that somebody up the chain of command is involved in this or, worse yet, is involved in the attempted murder of Mason."

Masters stared at him in shock. "Oh, hell no," he replied. "Those cases are the worst."

"I know it. As it turns out, Mason just came off an ugly scenario—and not long ago—where the commander of the base camp up in the Arctic was involved."

"Ah, shit," Masters mumbled, staring back at him in shock. "I hadn't heard."

"I'm not surprised. The brass likes to keep those things under wraps. The very nature of it doesn't inspire confidence in the troops or their leadership, and that is paramount."

"Of course." Masters considered all the implications of something like that and winced. "What a shitty thought."

"It's beyond shitty," Jasper confirmed.

Masters asked, "So do we know that Mason's case has some long arms, reaching out to get payback?"

"No, we don't know. And yet that is always possible,"

Jasper muttered. "I would hate to think so, but I'm not ready to rule anything out. Let's get what we can for information on this Nicholas guy so far and see what else we can come up with."

As Jasper got up to walk out, Masters called him back. "How do you feel about their not saying anything about another investigator's disappearance?"

"Shitty," Jasper stated. "That stops now."

Masters snorted. "Says you."

"Yep, says me," he declared, with a sigh. "And I understand that we have our work cut out for us to get that attitude shut down, as we can't have that."

"No, we can't, but it doesn't mean that any of them will be interested in talking to us about it."

"They don't have to talk to us," Jasper pointed out, with a flat smile. "They just have to do what they're told."

"Did you officially step in and take over this department?" Masters asked.

"It's in the works. I told the brass that I would handle this because of Mason, but I wasn't sure I wanted it long-term."

"I can't see the brass letting you do that, just taking the job on a contingency basis like that."

"They're not. So, yes, I did promise them more, but that doesn't mean I have any intention of solving everything else that this department is currently working on," he explained. "Yet I'm thinking about it."

"This is where you want to be though, right?"

"It is where I want to be, but I also want to ensure that the members of this department are people I could work with and handle, where the bosses won't be screwing me over every time I turn around."

"Ha. You find a department like that in the military, and I'll follow you right into it."

"I wanted to ask you earlier if you were interested in working as an investigator," Jasper noted. "We already have some staffing issues, as you can see."

"There are, indeed. Sam being one. What's up with that?"

"Apparently he's got a chip on his shoulder about other people making decisions without his input. Then add that to the fact that he's got ongoing issues with alcohol abuse, and it's a tough deal. I'll look into it more, but I get the sense that he goes for long periods of time being sober and doing well, but occasionally something will set him off, and he falls off the wagon."

"None of that will bode well for him in the military, particularly in the work we do."

"I know, and I plan to watch him pretty closely, so I can decide for myself. In the meantime, I'm cutting him a bit of slack and withholding judgment for a time," Jasper shared. "So, for the moment, he's free and clear to continue doing his job."

"Speaking of which, we have some information to track down," Masters said, tapping the computer screen.

"What did you find?"

"Nicholas has a sister."

"Interesting. And what about her?"

"Apparently she's the one who raised the alarm that he was missing, telling his team. Then she went to the brass, and afterward she contacted lawyers."

"Lawyers?" Jasper repeated, his eyebrows going up.

Masters nodded, as he read the sheet in front of him. "According to this, she maintains that the military has been no help in finding her brother and is directly responsible for what happened to him."

"Does she give any more information?"

"She does not." He got out a notepad, quickly wrote down her contact information and physical address, then looked over at Jasper and smiled. "Time for a road trip."

"It's definitely time to connect with somebody much more interested in Nicholas disappearing than anyone we've spoken to so far," Jasper replied, with a nod. "What's her name?" he asked curiously. "I may know her."

"Do you know many people around here?"

He shrugged. "Not that many, but it's always amazing how many people you do know after a few years in the navy," he commented.

"Let's see here. Her name is Elizabeth," he shared, reading it off from the page. "Elizabeth Woodrow."

"So, she's not married then?"

"No, not unless she just chose to keep her maiden name. It doesn't look like it, but I can't tell for sure. I don't have much history here on her," he said, clearing the screen and checking for more information. Then he shrugged. "Jeez, I'm not getting any information on her at all."

"Okay, we definitely need to give her a phone call then."

"It might be easier if I skip the phone call and go straight to a visit," Masters offered.

"That certainly cuts through a lot of the time-wasting, especially if she's fed up and wants to avoid that too."

"And we don't have time for any of that," Masters agreed, as he stood up. "Okay then, I'm out of here. So here's your desk back."

"Right, and make sure you follow through with getting that log-in resolved and anything else you need. Anybody gives you trouble, give me a shout."

"I'll work on it," Masters said, with a laugh. And, with that, he headed out to the parking lot and his car.

ELIZABETH WOODROW OPENED her front door and stared at the stranger with a look of consternation. "Can I help you?" she asked cautiously, looking around to see where this tall, incredibly capable-looking man had come from, wondering what the heck he wanted with her. He smiled at her in a gentle way that made her even more cautious. She shook her head. "I don't know you, and I don't understand why you're here, so please state your business, then be on your way."

His eyebrows shot up, and he nodded. "I'm investigating a possible murder attempt at the base."

Her stomach clenched, and all the heat sank to her toes, leaving her body chilled and trembling.

He made an odd exclamation and stepped forward, catching her as she stumbled into the small chair sitting outside on her deck. "I am so sorry," he blurted out. "It's not your brother. We didn't find your brother. It's not about him. Christ, I'm sorry. I should have made that clear."

She blinked rapidly, as the world started to refocus again. "Oh my God, are you sure?"

"I'm sure," he stated. "I'm here regarding a sniper shooting incident on the base," he added. "It has not resulted in a death at this time," he explained, "and we're doing everything we can to prevent that from happening."

She gripped the armrests of her chair and glared up at him. "None of that makes any sense."

"That's because I got off on the wrong foot with you and screwed up my response. I'm so sorry. Let me start over." Taking a deep breath, he began again. "We had an assassination attempt, a sniper shooting, on a fairly high-ranking officer on the base. It is still unclear if he will survive. We're figuring out who is behind it and why, and we've also had some additional attempts to take out people close to him, almost spitefully so because they failed at their first attempt on their intended target." He crouched in front of her, gripped her hands, and added, "I came because I don't know if this is connected in any way to your brother's disappearance."

She blinked. "And how would anybody know?" she snapped, some of her feistiness returning. "Near as I can tell, they did essentially no investigation into my brother's disappearance. So why the hell should I help you right now?"

"I understand how you could feel that way," he admitted. "And I'm certainly not here to tell you that everything was done as it should have been because I don't know that. I only just found out about your brother's disappearance and have just joined that department," he shared. "I can understand that you might be feeling a little bit bitter."

"A little bit?" she snapped again, glaring at him.

He winced. "Okay, so a lot, and I get that. However, if these cases are connected, it will help us to get answers for your brother."

She stared at him. "Yet somehow I suspect that the only answers we'll get involve the cases that you're actively investigating."

"It is a possibility, and I don't know for sure what has been done to date on your brother's case."

She shook her head, closed her eyes, and whispered to

herself that she could do this, that she *had* to do this. If nothing else, she had to do it for her brother. Nicholas was a good man. He didn't deserve to be dropped off into the abyss and forgotten. She finally opened her eyes to see the stranger staring at her in concern. "I'm fine," she whispered. "I'm not *fine*-fine but—"

"I understand," he replied. "I considered calling you first, but I was afraid you wouldn't talk to me."

She blinked her eyes at him several times. "Maybe I wouldn't have. I'm feeling pretty let down by the world, and I don't like the idea of talking to anybody."

"And yet, if we were able to do something to help find Nicholas, it could—"

"I would do anything for answers," she whispered. "Yet, so far, answers have been few and far between."

"Can you give me the details of what happened?"

She shrugged and began, "He … was having a regular week, and then, the day before he disappeared, he sounded a little stressed, a little worried. I talked to him that night, told him to go to bed and to get some sleep, and, when he woke up, things may not seem quite so difficult."

"Did he explain what the problem was?" Masters asked.

She slowly shook her head. "No, he didn't give me any details. Something about one of the cases he was working on. He couldn't get anywhere with it, and that was frustrating him."

At that, the stranger just nodded.

She frowned and asked, "Do you have any identification?" She knew nothing about this man. He pulled out his credentials, and she read the name on it. "Masters Woodrow. *Woodrow?*"

"I know, right, but no relation," he replied. "At least

none that I know of."

She nodded but continued to stare down at his ID. "That is an awfully odd coincidence."

"I was working on the sniper case before I found out about your brother's disappearance, so it's exactly what it sounds like, a coincidence."

She returned his ID and nodded, studying him through her narrowed gaze. "I can't say you look like the family."

"No, I don't," he agreed. "I'm dark-haired, and you guys are all, I presume, redheads."

"Yes. All of us are gingers, and we pay the price for that too," she shared, with an eye roll.

"I'm sorry," Masters replied. "Kids can be especially cruel."

"And I couldn't care less about any of that. I just want my brother back," she murmured. "He's all I have," she shared, looking over at him and holding back the tears.

He nodded. "I'm sorry."

"You don't think there's any hope of finding him alive, do you?"

He sighed. "I honestly have no idea because I'm just coming on this case, and I only learned about your brother today. However, I always approach cases like this with hope," he told her, "and can't imagine even doing this job without it."

She knew what he was saying, and he was right. But it all felt so very hopeless. "I pray you're right," she murmured. "It seems as if, up until this point, nobody has given a damn."

"Some of us do," Masters murmured. "And, right now, I need as many details as I can get. So can you go back to what you were saying?"

She nodded and picked up the story. "I talked with him

that previous night for, I don't know, maybe twenty or thirty minutes. He was obviously upset, though I wouldn't have thought he was terribly distraught or anything. *Frustrated* maybe is a better word," she stated, thinking about it.

"And he went to work the next day?"

"As far as I know, he went to work the next day as usual. He doesn't live here with me, but, when he didn't show up at the base, I was called because I'm listed as his contact. They asked if I had seen him, and I said no. Of course, that set me off, and I started calling Nicholas but got no answer," she shared, with a shrug. "And there's been no answer ever since."

Masters sat back on his heels, his arms resting easily on his knees as he stared at her. "And there has been nothing since that time?"

"There's been nothing ever again. I'm still waiting for him to show up to work or to come home from work, like nothing ever happened," she murmured. "I'm caught in limbo and getting absolutely nowhere."

"And I understand how unbelievably difficult that is."

"It sure is," she declared. "There's no closure in something like this, and you just … you're waiting. Every time you hear a knock at the door, every time you hear a noise, every time you hear a sound, you're just waiting for something, for anything to help you understand what happened. I'm still waiting for Nicholas to walk in the door. So far, he hasn't, and all that stressful and worrisome waiting continues."

He nodded and didn't say anything more.

"What are you thinking?" she asked, curious.

"I'm just wondering about all the various scenarios where something like that could have happened."

"You can wonder all you like," she said. "I've done more than enough wondering for a lifetime. It's never easy to *not* have any answers, and it doesn't seem to ever go away."

"No, of course not. So, you've tried his phone again recently?"

"Yes, but it just goes to voice mail. I don't know whether anyone from your team has contacted somebody to get the telephone records or if it's even trackable, but I would assume so. Nobody's told me whether they have or haven't, even though I've asked."

"So, I heard you got yourself a lawyer," Masters shared, a note of humor in his voice. When she eyed him suspiciously, he just shrugged. "I have to admire you for that," he said.

She snorted. "It didn't help. The military closed ranks, and, as far as they're concerned, it's an internal investigation, and it's still ongoing. It doesn't matter whether I like the way they're doing it or not. I don't have any say in the matter," she muttered. "And that's equally frustrating."

"I understand that for sure," he replied. "So, for the moment, we'll go on the assumption that he's alive. Do you know what case he was working on?"

She shook her head. "No, I sure don't. His investigations were something he took very seriously, and he held all to be very private in nature. I know that he was bothered about some aspect of his job, but he just wouldn't tell me very much."

"Depending on the circumstances, it would make sense that he couldn't share much with you."

"If you say so," she muttered. "At the moment, I wish he'd spilled the beans because, if it has anything to do with why he hasn't come home, I want to make sure that somebody pays the price for whatever has happened to him."

"I get it." He straightened and added, "I don't have legal access to his place. Do you still have it?"

"The mortgage is still paid out of his paycheck," she stated. "I'm the acting executor of his estate, but I can't do anything one way or another right now, and I don't want to do anything, … not until I know exactly what happened to Nicholas."

"Is there any way I could go to his house and take a look?"

Surprised, she slowly stood. "Yes, I guess so. What will that do?"

"It might not do anything," he conceded, "and I would hate to give you the idea that it could, but I've got to start somewhere, and who knows? Something at his house might help. After all, I won't know what I'm looking for until I find it."

"Then let's go," she stated abruptly. When he nodded, she shrugged. "He lived—he lives just around the corner."

"Let's go," he replied.

She pointed to her house. "Let me just grab my keys and his." And, with that, she headed back into her house. When she rejoined him, he stood there, staring around at the neighborhood. "Problems?" she asked.

"No, not at all," he said, "just checking out the area and what it's like here. Is there a high-crime rate or anything that would be disturbing?"

"No," she replied. "It doesn't make any sense that anything could have happened to him here. I walk constantly all over this place."

"Do you still do that though?" he asked, looking at her in surprise.

She nodded. "We've been here all our adult lives. I

bought this house, and he bought the house just down the road here," she explained. "So, this is a place we've always felt safe, and I can't imagine that would have ever changed for him. I've just assumed his disappearance had something to do with his work."

"And it could have. I'm not saying it doesn't. I just … don't know yet."

She studied him for a long moment, not exactly sure how to take this new arrival into her world, and then she shrugged. "Come on. Let's go. I'll take you over to the house." Leading the way, she headed out to Nicholas's house. As she got up to the front yard, she motioned at the door. "This is his place."

Masters stopped, took a good look around outside— something else that surprised her—then nodded and strode forward again.

"What did that little search do for you?" she wondered out loud.

He smiled. "Just getting a feel for the place," he murmured. "Things are always going on in life that you can't *place*, so you hope that something will make it feel right in some weird way."

She shrugged, not sure what that meant, but happy enough to let it go. She walked up to the front door, unlocked it, then stepped off to the side so he could take a look inside.

He stepped forward and asked, "Do you mind if I go in alone?"

Her eyebrows shot up, and she frowned.

"That's fine. Obviously my request bothers you. So your answer can be a no, if that's how you feel."

She didn't know what to say, but his request seemed odd

to her. She hesitated, watching from the sideline as he stopped at the entrance, almost as if just looking inside would tell him something important. She'd never seen anybody act like this before. His gaze never rested and went from the weird hall tree that her brother had for hanging coats, to the pictures on the wall and on from there, covering basically all of what could be seen from the front door.

She finally granted her permission for him to enter.

Masters moved from one thing to the other to the other.

Fascinated by him and encouraged by the thought that the military would do something this time, Elizabeth watched, as he worked his way through the first floor of her brother's home. When he finally came to a stop, she asked, "And?"

He smiled but shook his head. "I'm not seeing anything. You're right. However, I'm not saying there isn't anything to see."

Confounded by his wording, she waited as he walked through the rest of the house.

When he was done, he came back outside and sat down on the deck beside her. "It doesn't look as if there's been anyone in or out of here recently."

"No, of course not. Why would there be?"

"Cleaning ladies, you, anybody?"

She shook her head. "No. No reason for it. My brother wasn't here, so no need for me to be here."

"Could somebody have come in and come out without anybody seeing?"

Surprised, she frowned. "In theory it's possible, but I haven't seen anybody."

"And you haven't noticed any changes, anything moved, or anything along that line since you were here last?"

She curiously turned to look at the house behind them and asked, "What exactly are you talking about?"

He tilted his head and then spoke. "I don't see any electronics. I don't see a laptop. I don't see a desktop. I don't see a cell phone or chargers."

She stared at him, then blinked and nodded. "They were here, although surely Nicholas had a cell phone on him. I know the military took a lot of his electronics from here," she said cautiously. "They told me that they needed it for their investigation."

"And they probably would have taken Nicholas's electronics as part of their investigation," he agreed.

"*Probably would have* does not have the same meaning as *I would have expected it* or something like that."

He chuckled. "I'm not trying to split hairs with you or anything like that. If the base has Nicholas's electronics, I'll see if I can get access to them."

"I would hope so." When he glanced back at the house, she noted, "Something's bothering you."

"I guess it's the open window," he shared, with a wry look. "For me, I leave the windows closed most of the time. I have them open when I'm at home, but I close them when I'm gone, just because it's an open invitation for people."

"His windows are closed," she stated.

He studied her curiously, then shrugged. "They aren't though, are they?"

She let out her breath slowly. "Could you explain that, please?"

"Let me show you instead." And, with that, he got up and walked back into the house, and she followed.

Sure enough, in her brother's office, the window was open, and the curtains billowed freely. She shook her head.

"It never was open before," she exclaimed, as she raced over.

He stood in the doorway, as she turned and glared at him. "You saw that right away, didn't you?"

He shrugged. "I saw that the window was open right away, sure. The curtain is blowing everywhere, so why wouldn't I see that?" he asked, looking at her steadily. "The question is whether that's normal for him or not."

"It's not," she admitted. "Not at all."

"Okay. So, in that case, this is obviously something that's most likely changed, but, when it changed, I don't know."

She let out a deep breath, as she tried to think clearly. "It's very confusing because I didn't notice it. I wish now that I had."

"How often do you come over here?"

She frowned. "Lately not that often. After he first went missing, it was almost a daily occurrence. I couldn't leave it. I finally spoke to a therapist who seemed to feel that wasn't healthy for me."

"Wasn't healthy?" he repeated.

"Yes, because I was incapable of moving on," she explained. "It wasn't healthy, and I needed to let it go."

"Ha," he muttered. "That sounds like a therapist for you."

She smiled. "It does, doesn't it?"

He just nodded and didn't say more.

She had to admit that an awful lot of what the therapist had said didn't make sense to Elizabeth because seeing her brother, being close to her brother, had brought her comfort that was hard for anybody else to understand. Yet Masters here seemed to get it. She frowned at that too, not liking the way her thoughts were going or that this guy could understand what she was going through. "Have you ever lost anybody like this?" she asked.

"Like this? No," he replied. "This? … This is one of those experiences that you hope you never have to deal with. As you mentioned, there are just no answers, and you can't find any answers to make peace with your life. Therefore, it's hard to move on."

"Exactly," she agreed, "and that's probably why my therapist told me to find another way to make peace."

"And yet it didn't work."

"No, it didn't," she stated, with a nod. "Doesn't mean it couldn't work though. I'm just"—she winced—"I'm refusing to allow it to work."

He chuckled at that. "If it were my brother, my sister, my family, I would be right there with you."

Somehow it made her feel a whole lot better to know that he wasn't judging her for her actions and for her inability to let go. "She says it's not healthy."

"Maybe she's right," he said, with a shrug. "But it's not as if we can pick and choose our emotions for this thing, and I don't imagine that she knows what advice to give you, as it's not the easiest situation to deal with. What is she supposed to tell you? Just forget your brother? No. Honor your brother? How do you honor your brother when you don't even know if he's alive or dead?"

Elizabeth had to admit that, with every word Masters spoke, she felt a lot more relaxed and comfortable. She now had some hope that maybe the navy's investigation team would take her brother's case seriously after all.

As they walked through her brother's house again, he pointed at the kitchen and asked, "Does he always keep these windows closed?"

She nodded. "Yes, he does. He doesn't open the windows very often at all." She frowned and then added, "To be honest, he's a bit of a security freak."

At that, Masters slowly turned and nodded. "As an investigator, that could come with the job. Has he always been that way?"

She shook her head. "No, it was a more recent thing. He was looking into getting a better security system put in, and I didn't understand why. Honestly I'd forgotten about it until just now," she muttered. "I'm wondering if more was involved with that."

"It's possible," he said, "but you can't hold yourself responsible for that too."

At the word *too*, she turned, but he was staring straight at her, with that same calm, caring, and yet, not neutral, but almost implacable look. She'd never seen anything like it. "You said *too*."

"Haven't you taken on the guilt? He's your younger brother, isn't he?"

She held her breath, then let it out slowly and nodded. "Yes, he is my younger brother, and you're right. To some extent I feel terribly guilty."

"Do you want to tell me about that?"

"Not really, because it just adds to my guilt."

He smiled and said ever-so-softly, "All the more reason to find a way to get past it."

She sighed. "That night he wanted to talk, and I brushed him off," she admitted. "I was tired and stressed. I was beyond tired, to be honest. So, I talked to him for a little while, and then I shut him down. Now I wish I hadn't, and it's so frustrating because I never got a chance to say, *Hey, sorry about that* or to let him know that I did care, and that I wasn't just fobbing him off."

"I highly doubt that would be his reaction," Masters replied. "If it had been my sister, I would understand. I would completely get that she loved me and was just having a bad day. Or maybe I just had crappy timing, which you and I both know happens more than we would like to think. Either way, I'm pretty sure he would understand."

"What if he's dead, and that's just all that there is?" she murmured.

"If he's dead, and that's what's left, then that's the part you'll have to deal with. Yet don't take on the guilt because you didn't have time to talk to him very long. You did talk to him, even if it wasn't for very long."

"I did get a chance to tell him that I love him," she whispered. "I have to hang on to that."

"You do, and I wouldn't give up on him and assume that he's dead at this point either. We don't know yet, and we can't know. So, for the love of God, let's not put those thoughts and ideas into our reality one second before we have to."

Her lips twitched. "You sound very esoteric with that comment."

He shrugged. "I certainly didn't mean to. I'm just somebody who likes to see reality and not necessarily jump into other theories sooner than necessary. If he's dead and gone, you could have done nothing anyway. It most likely would have happened right around the time he went missing, and, if he's alive, then we'll find him."

"If he's alive, we should have found him a long time ago."

"Maybe, yet perhaps there's a reason why we haven't." He hesitated and then added, "Look. I know this sounds foolish, but did you check all the hospitals around here to confirm he wasn't there, even as a John Doe?"

"I phoned a bunch of local places early on, but I can't say I phoned everywhere. Is that—" Then she stopped and nodded. "I should make more phone calls, shouldn't I?"

"Let me get into it," he offered. "Let me put out some feelers and see if we can come up with something." He stopped, then asked, "By the way, what do you do for a living?"

"I'm in the finance industry. I work for a bank doing investments." He didn't say anything for the moment, then she lifted her gaze and asked, "Why?"

"Have you been approached in any way, in any unorthodox way?"

Her eyes widened. "I'm not sure I like the way you asked that. What exactly do you mean?"

"If we look at Nicholas's disappearance with an open mind, embracing all possibilities, we should consider the idea that he could have been taken and held because somebody wanted you to do something for them, and he'll be the trump card."

The breath whooshed out of her, as she stared at him in shock. "No, nothing like that."

He lifted a hand. "I'm not putting that idea out there as something that I'm considering either. I just … I can't *not* think about it when we have this scenario going on. If he had been missing for a shorter time period, and you got calls early on, then it would seem to be more of a possibility. However, the fact that he's been missing as long as he has makes this theory much less likely."

Dazed, she could only stare at him and slowly nod. "I do hope you're right," she whispered, "because that would be unbearable."

CHAPTER 2

ELIZABETH SAT ON a chair on her front porch, staring toward her brother's house. Ever since Masters left, she'd been unable to think of anything else. How had she missed the signs? How had she been so caught up in everything else going on that she hadn't seen a simple thing such as his home office window was open? How long had it been open, and who had opened it? The never-ending cycle of her thoughts tormented her, taking her down a darker and deeper avenue. Was there any chance that her brother was being held hostage? Had somebody kept him and not contacted her? Or had she been contacted but hadn't recognized it for what it was?

She racked her brain to find anything that would make sense, and yet nothing did. She would do anything to get her brother back and admitted that, over time, it had been a much harder concept to keep positive about. Yet the minute Masters had mentioned kidnapping, she couldn't stop wondering if that were possible, if Nicholas was still out there somewhere, still alive. And, if he was, could this be all about her?

The thought that it could be possible was absolutely stunning. She hadn't considered it for a single moment because she had automatically assumed his disappearance was related to his job and nothing else. The possibility of other options just hadn't occurred to her because of the work he did. He was all about safety and seemed almost inherently cautious, and his job alone made him feel that way more often than not. He'd once told her that he didn't think it was good for his psyche in many ways.

His investigations made him very wary of the outside world because even the most unassuming casual person could end up being a criminal who had absolutely no conscience. She remembered various tales he had told her about over the last couple years, though none of the details were clear enough that she could pinpoint what was fully going on—just enough to give her an idea of how crazy people were. Some of his cases had sounded extremely dangerous, implausible even. At one point in time, she thought he'd been making it up, only to realize he had been deadly serious.

Another time she even tried to get him to quit, to change jobs, to find something that was less psychologically damaging, but he'd replied that it was the only work for him. And she had believed him because he clearly lived for it. Yet it had potentially claimed his life. And, if not his life, then his freedom. The thought that he could have been suffering for all these months and was out there and nobody knew where was absolutely devastating.

She finally got up from the chair on her front porch, moving slowly in the chill of the outside air, and walked into her living room.

Just having the two of them in their family, she often wondered if they were both destined to be alone all the time. She'd had a couple relationships, and so had he, but nothing had lasted, nothing had made her want in any way to choose someone on a long-term basis. She'd often commented to Nicholas that maybe they were just too close, and he just shook his head and stated that being close as brother and sister had nothing to do with it. If that made somebody else not like their relationship, then they were threatened by all the wrong things.

She often agreed with him, but now it was hard to be alone, completely alone, with her brother not here—or anybody else who gave a crap about her, for that matter. That was one of the hardest things for her to understand right now. She'd never considered that her life was limited in any way, but, now that she didn't have her brother here with her, it was hard not to wonder if she had deliberately pushed away other people because she was content in her happy little bubble with Nicholas. She'd always thought that whenever that happy little bubble became something that she was willing to enlarge, then it would signify true love.

But, in the meantime, true love didn't appear, and she hadn't been saddened by the circumstances, still content with the bubble around her.

With a sigh, she made herself a simple dinner and sat down at her computer, wondering how she could possibly find out anything. She'd racked her brain for what seemed like forever, wondering what had happened to Nicholas in the first place, and had come up blank. And although the navy had told her that they were working on it, she had to question that.

Would they have done anything if this Mason person hadn't been attacked? She felt so sorry for him, and she certainly didn't want his family to go through anything like what she had. While Mason at least had been rescued, she didn't know whether he had survived or not. She tried to look up news on that but couldn't find very much. She figured the military probably kept a media blackout on it in order to keep a handle on the stories that the public came across. After all, their investigation continued on that Mason shooting. Maybe they had done that blackout for her brother's case too. She just didn't know.

With a glass of lemonade, she went back outside, this time sitting on her backyard porch swing, watching as the sun slowly sank down behind the mountains. She wasn't even sure she would sleep tonight, not with so much going on in her world. The more she thought about that stupid open window in Nicholas's house, the more it made her angry, the more it made her feel like she hadn't paid attention, that she had missed something.

She tossed back the last of her lemonade, got up, grabbed the keys to her brother's house, and walked back over there again. It was only a few minutes away and made it an easy trip. Yet it also made her angry because, if something had been going on, she should have seen it, and she should have recognized the inherent trouble. What was the point of looking after each other's houses, if you didn't even see trouble when it approached? She knew a lot of people were quick to let her off the hook, but she wasn't so sure she should be because right now it was just bizarre.

As she walked along the sidewalk, Dolly called out to Elizabeth. Dolly was at least seventy-something and had lived here most of her life. When Elizabeth lifted her hand and waved, Dolly motioned for her to come over.

Elizabeth called back, "I'll stop by on my way back."

Dolly let her hand drop to her lap and just waited.

She was good at that. She sat on her porch for what

seemed like a lifetime, just waiting, waiting for whatever happened next in her world. In her case, considering the fact that she didn't do anything to change her world, chances were, it was just one more step closer to dying.

That was a terribly maudlin thing for Elizabeth to consider, but, ever since her brother had gone missing, it was just the way she felt. Inside her brother's house, she slowly walked around again, checking out everything she had seen with Masters, yet nothing else came to light. Nothing looked any different. Nothing looked any better or any worse. She went through his bedroom again, searching for any inkling of something that was different, something that would provide answers.

If he was being held captive, why? And, if he was still alive, where the hell could he possibly be, and would anything in his house let her know? Going through his place with much more intent, she headed to his closet, opened it up, and stared at his clothing. His organized closet was so typical of him, it was pretty tidy, with clothes hung up by color, mostly dark. When not required to be in uniform, he wore a lot of sport coats and jeans, as well as simple T-shirts and jeans. He had been—no, he *is*, she corrected herself—a simple man with simple tastes, seeking the simple joys in life.

It all made tears come to her eyes, as she thought about him. He was a good person, *is* a good person, and whatever he'd been working on, whatever had been bothering him, could easily have been work-related. It even could have had something to do with his personal life that he hadn't told her about. It was quite possible that something or someone was in his life. Because of their multiple failed relationships, and her own comments about their being too close, maybe he now kept things to himself a little longer, not wanting to share until it became something or became nothing.

She'd done the same herself a time or two. Even as she checked out all Nicholas's clothing, she couldn't see anything hidden, anything different, anything other than her normal upstanding brother. Frowning, she checked the wood board at the bottom of the closet, holding his shoes and boots. It did protect the carpet there but … Now curious, she removed the shoes and tugged at the board. Beneath it were envelopes, some small and white, some larger and brown. Taking a closer look, absolutely nothing seemed suspicious about the standard Number 10 envelopes. Inside she found letters, with family photos, which she found oddly touching.

With just the two of them left in the family, he had saved pictures of their father and mother in various places and poses—and their baby pictures, which she appreciated, because these were photos that she wasn't even sure existed.

The second set of 9x12 brown envelopes were more of a mystery, and there were a few of them. And yet they looked, … she hesitated and then filled in what her mind had refused to acknowledge. They looked more ominous. They looked more professional, as in legal papers. Taking a breath, she opened the first one to find a will. Not surprisingly, as she read the will, he'd left everything to her. It's also what her will set forth. Everything she had was to go to her brother, if she died before him.

She stared at the proof of his love for her, knowing that no way he would even let her see this if he could be here. It tore her apart to think that this is where her life was going, a life without her brother. As she opened another brown envelope, it held more legal documents, this one involving investments. She was stunned at the amount of money he had accumulated.

It was more money than she'd even contemplated him having. Yet, according to the paperwork and her knowledge of financials, they were normal standard investments. And, of course, he hadn't spent much of his money when she thought about it. He worked all the time, including a lot of overtime, but still, he had amassed a lot of money.

Frowning, she put that envelope down and grabbed another one. This one held more investments. Curious, and more than a little worried, she reached for her phone and the business card that Masters had left behind. When he answered, his tone slightly stiff, as he seemed to be busy, and she was interrupting him. "Look. I … It doesn't matter."

"It matters," he replied. "What's up?"

Again she opened her mouth to explain but then hesitated.

"Want me to come over?"

"No, no, no, that's not fair to you. And honestly this isn't fair to my brother."

"This isn't about fairness," he stated.

She heard sounds in the background.

"I'm already heading to my car. I'll be there in just a few minutes."

"Are you sure?" she asked. "It's probably nothing."

"I've heard that a time or two also," he noted. "Let's hope it is nothing."

"Right," she said, with relief. "That's, that's exactly what I am hoping. I'm at my brother's house."

"Good. I'll be there as quick as I can." Then he disconnected.

She stared down at the other paperwork. She wasn't at all sure that she should continue to even look further. It felt as if she were defiling something special, something personal of his, and she didn't want to do that. She didn't want to invade, and she didn't want to intrude. Yet what else was she supposed to do right now? If he was dead and gone, did any of this have something to do with his disappearance and later passing?

She didn't want to think so, but she also couldn't understand what had happened to him or why. Plus, if his disappearance was all about his job, was any of this about his job, or was it about his private life? She didn't know. She picked up the next brown envelope, and it seemed completely empty, but, as she turned it upside down, a small metal item fell out, shaped like a decorative key ring, a memento from a trip to Mexico or wherever. She picked it up and stared at it, her heart sinking because this was a USB drive. And that could turn this whole investigation in a different route.

MASTERS DROVE UP and parked outside Nicholas Woodrow's home. As he walked up to the front door, it opened in front of him, and Elizabeth, pale, her lips pinched together, waved to a woman across the road, and then motioned him inside. "Who was that?" he asked.

"An old lady who watches the neighborhood," she replied. "I promised her that I would stop by after I was done over here."

He looked back out at the old lady who was watching the house with interest. "I know you probably don't want to bring it up," he began, "but is there any chance she might have seen anything to do with your brother?"

She appeared startled and shook her head. "Even if she

did, she's not always quite there."

"But often, *not quite there* isn't the same as not being there," he reminded her. "And I hate to say that we're desperate for information, but—"

"But you're desperate for information," she broke in. She hesitated, then shrugged. "I can talk to her. I don't have a problem with that. Everybody in the neighborhood knows that my brother is missing," she stated. "Not to mention I put up posters and all kinds of circulars to try and get anybody with any information to speak up."

"Would she have seen them?"

"I don't know," she replied, frowning at him. "I would have thought so, but she doesn't get out much, so maybe not."

"And enough time has gone by, so, if anything scared her, she might be willing to talk now."

"But that would imply a reason why she wouldn't talk back then," she pointed out.

"There are all kinds of reasons why people don't want to talk," he stated. "Even if it could be helpful. Sometimes their reasons don't make sense to us."

"If she's been harboring any information that could help solve my brother's disappearance," she said, "I would very much like to know what reason that could be."

"It could just be a fear of getting involved," he noted. "Now I came for a reason. What was that about?"

"Oh, sorry." She shook her head. "Follow me."

He followed her to her brother's bedroom, and, when they got there, he stopped to see several envelopes on the bed. He walked forward and asked, "Where did you find these?"

She pointed to the bottom of the closet. "Under that

piece of wood, where he had all his shoes and boots."

He checked under the wood and found nothing else. He looked back at her. "What's in the envelopes?"

"Some things make sense. His will, family mementos, photos, things like that," she began. "But something that I had absolutely no idea about, and I don't know if it is in any way connected, was his financial portfolio. I had no idea he had that money."

"And when you say *that* money, what does that mean?" When she hesitated, he added, "Look. I don't care how much money you brother had, unless it's related to his disappearance." He frowned. "Unless those financial documents raise red flags in your opinion, based on your experience."

She nodded. "Millions. He had millions."

At that, his eyebrows shot up. "Do you have any idea how or why?"

"No. Despite my job as a financial advisor, we never talked about stuff like that," she cried out. "This is personal. These are his finances. That's why I feel like I'm doing him a complete disservice by even looking at them or bringing it up."

"Okay, but you're only talking about it. You're not accusing him of anything. So, if he came by these millions through his investments or any other profits, that's totally legal," he noted. "That's not an issue. We just need to know if this is related to his disappearance. So, is there any chance that this money has to do with something illegal or that somebody else wants that money and they don't quite know how to get it? If so, then he could be held hostage until he willingly signs it over."

She stared at him blankly.

"I know that it may sound far-fetched, but—"

"No, no," she argued. "It doesn't sound all that far-fetched, and it's a hell of a lot nicer than anything else I've been thinking."

"And yet?"

"The thought of his being held hostage is absolutely disgusting, but the thought of his being alive and being able to recover from whatever asshole things they've done to him, that's a whole different story," she declared.

Masters looked down at the envelopes, some white, some brown.

She pointed to one stack of the 9x12 brown envelopes. "These are the investments. That stack of white envelopes is full of family mementos. But this brown envelope?" She hesitated and then opened it up so that he could look inside.

His eyebrows shot up. "A USB key."

"Yes, and that's when I got worried. The investments are not so much concerning as they were surprising. Yet it could easily have been good assets for him, and he did invest in several of his friends' companies," she shared. "I'd forgotten all about that until you said something. Now I'm thinking that could easily explain where he got the money."

"When you say, *his friends' companies*, what else do you remember about them?"

"He had some friends who were big into computer games, and they developed games and programs," she explained. "I remember him saying that he'd given them some money to get off the ground, so …"

He nodded. "So, venture capital. This could be fully legit, and it could very well mean that it was a good move and a nice thing in his life, so he can retire whenever he wants to."

"And I think he was getting to the point of thinking that retirement might be good, but yet *this*, whatever it was that was bothering him, truly *bothered* him."

"To the point that he wouldn't leave until it was settled?"

"I think so, but I think he also thought …" And she hesitated.

"What?" Masters asked.

"I think, and I have no way of knowing this, but I got the feeling that it may have been *final*."

At her wording, he stared at her.

"I don't mean *final*, like he'll die or something, but more like it might be the end of his career."

He sat back and studied her carefully. "And that would be pretty difficult for him to understand?"

"Not really. I think he understood the workings of his department quite well," she stated, "but I don't think … I think some things were *wrong* in that department."

His heart sank, as he heard echoes of Jasper's earlier words. "Maybe, but let's keep an open mind. Are you okay if I take this USB key?"

She winced. "I want a copy of it first."

He stared down at it and nodded. "I guess that's fair."

"It's my brother's property, and I don't know what it is or why he's got it, but I feel that I have to protect it."

"Do you have a computer here, anything I can copy it to?" he asked.

"Back at my place," she murmured.

"Okay, let's go." He stopped, then looked around. "Let's put the family photos back where you found them. And put his shoes back on top of it all. We don't want to alert anybody that we've been digging around in here. However, grab all the investment portfolio stuff."

"Any reason why?"

"Yeah, to keep it safe. And, if those mementos are important to you, better grab them too."

Frowning, she did as he asked, and he nodded.

"Depending on who these people are and how much they care about whatever information you may or may not have found, this house could be torched."

"Oh, shit," she muttered, as she held the mementos closer to her chest.

"It's just a precaution," he said. "Obviously we don't know for sure what's going on, but let's think far enough ahead and take this back to your home for safekeeping."

"I don't think your idea of thinking far enough ahead and mine are on the same plane," she replied in a slightly desperate tone. "That's not something I want to think about at all."

"I get that," he noted. "And yet, if it happens, you will thank me. And, if he comes back, you can just return it all to him. Will he be upset that you came in and looked at his stuff?"

She laughed. "He used to tell me that, if he was dead and gone, he was dead and gone. So, if I could use something, I should use it."

"Did you look at his will?"

She nodded. "I did, and I am sole inheritor of his estate."

He thought about that and what it would imply in other ways.

"So, yes, that puts me on the chopping block as suspect number one."

He nodded slowly. "As you are the only family member

left, and this is his estate, it would make sense that you would be a suspect. Have the police charged you with anything?"

"No, of course not," she declared bitterly.

"But you feel as if you're being judged in that way?" he asked cautiously.

"Sure I do. I think they decided it was all my fault and never investigated Nicholas's disappearance at all. In some ways they just don't believe me. Worse, they may think that I made a false report and that I killed him and know enough to do this in order to hide my tracks. I don't think the notion that he's gone missing and might need help has been given any credence because they think I killed my brother."

He whistled out loud at that. "That would be pretty terrible."

"That's just what I think of the people I spoke to," she stated, glaring at him. "The local cops and the military were both so dismissive. Or maybe it's just what I prefer to think so I don't have to question whether they are looking after their own. I thought the military never left anybody behind."

"Pretty sure that's the US Marines," he clarified, with a small smile. "Yet I do know what you mean. We are a unit, and that would be the standard practice."

She nodded. "Somebody should be looking for him."

"What was his relationship like," he asked, as he walked to the front door, "with the rest of his team?"

She shrugged. "He never talked about it, never talked about them, so it's hard to know."

"Maybe it's hard to know, but it's not impossible. I'm sure you have some idea."

"I'm not sure that I do," she clarified, looking at him. "It's not that I know anything. In fact, it may be more relevant that I don't."

He nodded. "But, over the years, even your intuition didn't pick up on anything?"

She winced. "Sure, yes, but I don't, I can't say that's anything I would put any faith into."

"I do," he declared. "I think intuition is very important." When she frowned at him, he smiled. "I know that makes for a fairly unpopular opinion, doesn't it?"

"I don't know about *unpopular*," she noted, "but it definitely puts you into the category of *different*."

"I'm okay with being different," he stated calmly.

"Did you always work in this investigative stuff?"

"Always? No, but, once I got into it, I realized I had a knack for it. So I've been there ever since," he explained. "However, I'm not officially on these cases yet."

"So, why are you here then?" she asked, frowning at him.

"I'm a special investigator, looking into Mason's case," he reminded her. "And I'm doing that as a friend, … for Jasper."

"Jasper, Jasper," she repeated, frowning. "I don't know that name."

"No, but you will," he replied comfortably. "He's a friend."

"And you guys do this stuff for friends?" she asked, astonished.

He chuckled. "You would be surprised how much we do for friends."

"No, I don't know that I would be surprised at all. I think that's what my brother always wanted, but he was … He was a little bit on the socially awkward side. He was a little bit on the OCD side."

He nodded. "So, you're saying he didn't have any friends

in the department."

She winced. "I hope that's not true. I would hope that people cared and that somebody saw the value that he brought to the job. But honestly I'm not sure they did."

Masters thought about how little he'd heard about Nicholas's disappearance case, how little information he'd been given, and realized that her take on it could be true. It would be sad if that were the issue, and Masters would be sure that wasn't the way it ended. And, for Nicholas, who had spent his life solving all these cases? Masters wanted to confirm that Nicholas got justice too. Or better yet, that he got his ass back home where he belonged.

"I'll take it under advisement, as they say," he added. "We'll follow up. Now let's get this back to your place, so I can get a copy of the USB, and so you can keep that other stuff safe." He hesitated as he walked by her side. "And please tell me, have you had any disturbances yourself?"

"What do you mean?" she asked.

"Any break-ins, any robberies, any strange events during the night, anything?"

She frowned and shook her head. "No, I wouldn't have. ... I can't remember anything."

"And you likely would remember if such a thing had happened?" he asked, cocking an eyebrow at her.

"Yes, I would think so. I'm not somebody who gets nervous easily," she shared, "although I have been a lot more nervous since my brother's disappearance."

"Which is to be expected," he confirmed. "And, if you had a problem before, you would have called your brother, I presume."

"Yes, exactly."

"You mentioned how you work for a bank. Did you

look at those investments of Nicholas's long enough to decipher anything about them?"

"No," she confessed, flushing. "It felt like I was intruding in his world."

"Do you think anything of concern is there?"

She shook her head. "No, but you're right. I should be the one who takes a good look at it."

"Then please do," he suggested, "but I do need a copy of the USB."

She groaned. "Why wasn't all this done before?"

"Because I don't think anybody found those envelopes," he guessed. "So, the question is, why did nobody find those? Maybe the real question is, where was this stuff when the original investigation was started?"

"I don't know," she murmured. "I don't, but you're making me more worried every time you open your mouth."

CHAPTER 3

ELIZABETH LOOKED OVER to see if Dolly was on her porch, but she wasn't. With a grateful sigh, Elizabeth raced on by.

When she and Masters were in the sanctuary of her home, he asked, "So, you didn't want anybody to see what we were carrying, or were you avoiding your neighbor?"

Surprised at his intuitiveness, she winced. "That doesn't sound very good, does it?"

"Not necessarily, but you told her that you would go see her. Is that something you're avoiding?"

"Maybe," she admitted. "I just don't want to be asked any questions right now."

"And yet it's a good time to ask questions of others," he pointed out.

"I know. I know." She raised her hands in frustration. "But all this has stirred up something that I don't have any answers for, so it's making me a little touchy." She walked into the kitchen and put on the teakettle. "You can use my laptop right there." She pointed to it.

And, with that, he turned it on and put the USB key in.

She stepped up behind him, waiting for the files to load, so she could read the contents too. It was only one file. As it popped up on the screen, it was labeled Evidence. "Ah, shit," she whispered.

Masters double-clicked it, and it opened to reveal other files and a lot of images. Masters clicked on one of the images.

She sucked in her breath. "Oh my God, is that a dead man?"

His voice grim, he nodded. "Maybe."

"Maybe?"

"I don't have any ID. I don't have any way to confirm that at the moment," he explained. "I'll get back to you on that."

"Shit," she muttered. "What was Nicholas into?"

"I don't know." Masters quickly copied the contents to her desktop and saved it and then shared, "I'm a little worried about your having this."

"It's my brother's, and, if he's dead, I get everything in his estate anyway," she stated bluntly. "And you're not taking a copy without my having a copy."

"And I don't have a problem with that, for sure," he told her. "I'm just worried about somebody finding out that *you* have it."

She froze as she understood what he was saying. "You're thinking it'll be dangerous for me."

"Your brother's disappeared, and he's worth millions of dollars. We don't know anything about where he's gone or why he's disappeared. Now we find he has a hidden file called Evidence. So I think it's safe to say, *Yes, if you have this info, you could be in danger.*"

She sucked in her breath and stared at him. "I appreciate the honesty," she began, "but, right now, it would be nice if you would say something like, *Hey, don't worry about it. This will all blow over, and you'll be totally fine.*"

But he stared at her steadily and did not give her that reassurance.

She sank into the kitchen chair beside him. "I should never have found this, should I?"

"It wasn't terribly well hidden, was it?"

She thought about it, then shrugged. "Under a piece of plywood, atop the carpet at the bottom of his closet? No, yet, in a way, yes. It was all filed, very methodically, like he is," she noted. "I would have expected him to have his things in order, one way or another. When he went missing, I called. I cried. I even got lawyers involved to get somebody to give a shit. The fact that Nicholas was one of the navy's own investigators just meant that they had locked everything down."

"And yet I'm getting the idea from you that maybe they didn't lock anything down."

Elizabeth added, her voice rising, "Look at how much time has been wasted, when they could have been actively looking for Nicholas. Maybe they didn't do any investigation."

Masters held up a hand and clarified, "That I can't confirm. I just know that I don't have full access to the investigation yet."

She shook her head. "And that's bullshit." He smiled as if appreciating her fury, but she wouldn't be appeased by something like that. "My brother deserves everything the navy can do for him," she declared, trying hard not to rant in his face. "He's a good man, and he needs help. He's either alive and needs help, or he was alive and needed help, and nobody was there for him."

"And you shouldn't feel guilty for anything he's gone

through," he stated firmly.

She snapped, "Of course I'm not guilty."

His lips twisted.

"Yet somehow I still feel guilty. Right. I know. I know. I know," she murmured, as she buried her face in her hands.

After a moment he grabbed her fingers and gently squeezed them. "Look. The files are transferred. I want you to hide them on your laptop somewhere or move them to cloud storage. Then delete this copy and restart your computer. Anybody who is any good with computers could still retrieve these files," he explained. "You've got to understand that. But you don't know anything about what's on them, and you need to keep it that way, right?"

"Yes," she agreed. "I didn't like anything about what you mentioned earlier. However, I will get a handle on his financials."

"Good. You do that part," he said. "And give me a heads-up when you get through it all."

"I will," she replied. She watched as he got up to leave.

Then he turned and suggested, "Hopefully you're having a nice cup of calming herbal tea right now and not more coffee."

She looked over at the teakettle. "If I was doing coffee, somebody should just shoot me now," she muttered. "Coffee is my absolute favorite all-time drink, but maybe not right now."

He smiled and nodded. "Just checking."

"I'm not that far gone," she muttered. She got up and walked him to the door, knowing that he had the USB key in his pocket, and she had the rest of the physical documents. "Do you think the documents are safe here?"

"No. My suggestion would be to put it all in a safe deposit box. At least until we can get through this. If we ever get his body, or we find him, you'll need those documents just to make your legal case," he explained. "So, be safe and take care of everything."

"Got it." She sighed. "You do realize I won't sleep tonight now."

"Neither will I. Neither will I." He turned to face her. "I know you don't need my number because you've got it in your phone already, but please make sure you've got a way to find my card in case you lose your cell or something," he suggested. "Call me if there's any problem."

"And when you say, *any problem*?" she asked, letting her voice trail off, studying his face.

"Any kind of problem. For all I know they're watching you right now, and now that they've seen me come here twice, they're wondering why."

"Maybe you should take everything then," she offered suddenly.

He frowned. "Are you that nervous?"

"You're certainly not doing anything to relieve that nervousness," she snapped.

"True," he muttered. "Do you have a safe deposit box?"

"I do, but I would have to get through the night in order to get this paperwork somewhere safe tomorrow," she explained, trying for humor, only to have it fall flat.

He hesitated. "So, how nervous are you about staying here alone tonight?"

She winced. "I wasn't before."

"And now you are," he noted, with a nod. "Okay, so how do you feel about an overnight houseguest?"

She stared at him. "Seriously?"

"You tell me. I'm fully prepared to stay here and to sleep

on the couch, so you can get a good night's sleep. Then we can get those documents to the bank first thing in the morning," he shared. "I also think you should be quick to put it all into a digital format, so you have that proof too. It's quite possible that, if Nicholas did invest in some of these companies, and he did make that money, maybe he also owns shares in those stocks, and people want his shares back. I don't know. I don't know anything about it, except that, right now, we've got a problem. Thus I would feel a whole lot better if all this was backed up somewhere."

"Well shit," she muttered, staring at him.

He nodded. "So what's the decision?"

She didn't even know what to say.

He nodded. "And your silence then is a decision."

"What decision?" she asked, with a note of humor.

"The decision is, I'm staying, so you need to put more water in the teakettle."

CHAPTER 4

ELIZABETH WOKE EARLY the next morning and hurried downstairs, hoping to be awake before her houseguest, but, of course, he was sitting in the kitchen on his phone. She looked over at him.

He smiled. "Good morning."

"At least we made it through the night," she noted, half joking.

"We did, indeed," he stated, with a smile. "How are you feeling?"

"I got some sleep, so I'm doing fine and feeling foolish."

He shook his head and added, "Hey, staying alive is never being foolish."

"Being paranoid is another story," she quipped.

He smiled at her. "So far I haven't seen anything bordering on paranoia, so I wouldn't worry about that."

"*Yet*, you mean."

He chuckled. "You can add *yet* if you want and if it makes you feel better, but honestly you're handling a lot of very difficult information pretty well."

She smiled at him. "I think you're one of those nice men who always tries to make life easier for people."

He laughed at that. "I know a lot of people who would

argue with you on that point. Remember how I'm one of the military investigators? I have to be a hard-ass at times, and that is rarely appreciated."

"No, it wouldn't be appreciated," she agreed, "but that doesn't mean that what you do is wrong. I know Nicholas always told me how his job alienated people in a way, and that wasn't fair to him either."

"No, it certainly wasn't, and it isn't, but it is the job," Masters stated firmly. "That's just part of it."

"Right. So …" She looked around and realized that a pot of coffee was dripping.

He apologized. "Sorry, I didn't know whether you would be upset that I took the liberty of making coffee or appreciate the fact that it's done and ready."

She laughed. "Because I'm desperately in need of coffee, I'll go with the latter."

"Good, I was hoping you would."

She poured two cups and brought them over, as he put down his phone. "Were you working?"

"Of course. I've contacted my boss as well."

She nodded. "Was he upset that you spent the night?"

"Why would he be upset?" he asked her in astonishment.

She flushed. "It just seems weird."

"It's not weird," he declared. "Stop thinking that you're being paranoid about this. This investigation is too important. Jasper was quite surprised at the documents you found too, and I have emailed copies of the file from the USB to him as well."

Elizabeth frowned, as she thought about the repercussions. "What if Nicholas wasn't even supposed to have those files?"

"Maybe he wasn't. It won't be common knowledge."

"Meaning?"

"Meaning that we will keep his USB files confidential at the moment, until we clear everybody in his department first. We must ensure that this isn't involved in the sniper case we're already dealing with."

She shook her head. "As much as I want all this solved, it never occurred to me that it would be this difficult."

"No, nobody ever thinks it'll be hard."

"Surely somebody knows who shot Mason, and so that's got be easy, right?"

Masters shrugged. "On TV they solve it within a half-hour show," he noted. "Real life isn't like that. You see those cold cases where they go twenty, thirty years, and then sometimes technology has improved enough that they can do something with the evidence. You just have to be grateful for the foresight of the people who collected all the evidence at the beginning and kept it, hoping that sometime down the road there would be technology that would help."

"That is one of the most fascinating aspects to me," she murmured. "That somebody thought far enough ahead to collect everything and then hoped technology would catch up someday."

"And now that is catching up," he pointed out. "We have more and more cold cases being solved, and sadly not always in time for the family of the victims to find closure. However, in many cases, it is in time for the culprits themselves to be captured."

"Can you imagine the criminal who, for that many years, thought they were free and clear, until suddenly one day they get caught? I'm sure it must be like a bolt out of the blue for them," she noted, shaking her head.

"I would imagine so. In many cases they're arrogant

enough to think that they didn't leave anything behind and that they're perfectly safe. They may spend that first year or two worrying about it, but then, to them, it's just a done deal."

She nodded. "I can't think of anything more satisfying than working on cold cases like that."

HE SMILED. "THAT'S a big part of it, but so is working on current cases." In fact, Masters loved his job. "My job is very fulfilling, yet frustrating, all at the same time," he shared, with a smile.

"And yet *do* you have a job?" she asked in a half-joking manner.

"I do. It's just that our investigative team works on different levels within the military, and not everybody knows all the details about what everybody else does," he murmured.

Maybe she didn't even know what he was doing. "So, now what?"

"Why don't we both run to your bank and put Nicholas's physical documents in your safe deposit box there? Have you got digital copies on your computer and in the cloud as well?" When she nodded, he added, "After that I'll drop you off and head back to my office and sort through the information on the USB drive. What about you and your work? Where should I drop you?" he asked curiously.

"I mostly work from home," she replied, looking around, frowning. "I only go in when I have a specific need to be there in person."

Thankfully the trip to the bank and back went without a hitch, although Elizabeth remained nervous, looking around at her surroundings, even when inside the bank.

"No one's following us," he shared, which seemed to calm her down on the way back to her house. He walked her to her door and went inside with her. After he checked out her house and all the windows and doors, he rejoined her in the kitchen. "I know it probably sounds autocratic, and I certainly don't mean it to because it's more about your safety, but could you check in with me, each time you come and go throughout the day?"

Her eyebrows slowly rose as she contemplated that. Then she studied his face and nodded. "Considering you stayed here overnight for me, that's the least I can do."

"At some point," he reminded her, "talk to your neighbor."

She hesitated and then sighed. "I probably should. If nothing else it'll encourage her to continue keeping an eye on Nicholas's property."

"That's not a bad thing right now," he pointed out.

She winced. "I don't want to think that I'm in any danger."

"I don't want to think that either," he murmured, "so let's not even go there."

"Wouldn't that be nice," she muttered, with half a laugh. "I guess it's all about sorting through what's going on and then coming to some understanding."

"It's a lot of things," he noted, "and we're missing a ton of information, but the bottom line is, we need to find out what happened to your brother, and we still need to sort out what is happening with Mason."

"Nicholas is my brother, so it's hard to even think that Mason's investigation is taking precedence over the disappearance of Nicholas," she admitted, "but I guess it's not so much that as the new versus old information involved."

"That's a good way to look at it," he pointed out. "Cold cases stay cold until something triggers a new lead. In this situation, Mason's case could be good for finding out more about your brother."

"In that case, I should reach out to the navy again."

"Or don't," he said, with a wry look. "Let's not have anybody think you guys are connected to the sniper shooting of Mason."

Astonished, she stared at him. "Seriously?"

"Yeah, seriously," he stated, "because we don't know what's going on here, not with Mason and not with Nicholas. Thus, we don't want anybody to start making assumptions. As investigators, we are looking for patterns, for connections, for who might have told something to whom, and you could end up on the chopping block next," he reminded her. "And that is something we don't want. … This may sound very *James Bond*-like, but I suggest we have a code word from you, where if anything were to happen and you needed to alert me, and only me, you could casually use that word. That way I would know you're in trouble. So then I would drop everything and ride to the rescue."

She snorted. "I've never had a code word. Although … my brother and I did something like that when we were kids, but it was more about having fun."

Masters nodded. "I'm not talking about fun right now. I'm talking about safety."

Her laughter died when she realized he was serious. She slowly nodded and added, "I'll use the same one we used back then—*ice cream*." When he laughed, she shrugged. "Whenever one of us was struggling with life, we used to ask about ice cream, so it became a code word of sorts. When times were tough, it meant I needed help. And often," she shared, with a smile. "Even as adults one of us would come over with ice cream."

"Good enough. So, if I happen to find Nicholas somewhere and told your brother that his sister has ice cream, would he recognize the reference?"

"Oh, absolutely," she declared, eyeing him. "It's funny how nobody else even thought to ask me something like that."

"No, of course not," Masters replied, his lips twitching, "because nobody was thinking along these lines. Since I'm expanding all aspects of the investigation, I want to find out what happened to him. If he's alive, let's get him back home, or, if he needs help, let's get him someplace where he can get it." After they shared a quick breakfast of toast and eggs, Masters departed. With a promise to check in, he left in his car and headed toward the office. As he walked in, Jasper was there, waiting for him. Masters motioned to Jasper's office. "Let's go in here and talk. You got coffee?"

"I've got coffee," he murmured, leading them both to the back office that Jasper still used. He closed the door and pointed to his own coffee machine. "Is it so bad that you need coffee?"

"It's not that it's so bad that I need coffee, just that I could use some more," Masters clarified, with a smile, already pouring a cup. "I did have two cups already though."

"Which is more than I expected you to get."

"Right? Anyway she's doing better this morning, not quite so worried, so I was glad to see that." He sighed, as he sat down. Taking a quick sip of coffee, he set his cup on Jasper's desk.

"Do you think there's any connection here?" Jasper

asked.

At that, Masters frowned, checking that the door was shut and that they had some privacy. "Any chance you've got any cockroaches around here?"

At that, Jasper's gaze narrowed, as he understood the reference. He walked over to the nearby closet, pulled out a small black box, and quickly did a sweep of the room. When no signal came that the room was bugged, he turned back to Masters. "Happy?"

"I'm happy that we checked," he replied. "And I'm happy that nothing is here right now. However, that is something you'll want to do on a regular basis."

Jasper grimaced. "I still haven't cleared everybody who works in this department." With that check done, and the black box returned to the closet, he sat down again and asked, "Did you have any particular reason for wanting that done?"

"No specific reason except that whatever was done with the initial investigation into Nicholas disappearing, nothing's been followed up on, at least not to the extent that it should have been," he stated in a low voice.

Even though they didn't find any bug, he wasn't at all assured that this room was not still compromised in another way. He just didn't have any way to check it out right now.

Jasper nodded. "I was wondering about that too. I looked at Nicholas's case file, and, while an investigation was done, it doesn't seem to have been done as thoroughly as you or I would have liked."

"Exactly, and we have somebody concerned that her brother's case was fobbed off for another reason."

"What reason would that be?" he asked curiously.

"That's what we don't know. Now, if you're about to

ask if I'm being influenced by feelings for her, the answer is no."

"I wouldn't say any such thing," Jasper noted in a mild tone, yet with a hint of a smile, "but now that you brought it up …"

"I spent the night, yes, and I slept on the couch. There is concerning information on this USB key."

"It's more than worrying." Jasper looked grim.

"You'll need to get the rest of this team checked out pretty damn fast," Masters muttered.

"I know it," Jasper replied, "and I would normally ask Tesla to look into something like this on a private level. However, … with everything going on—"

"I think you should still ask her," Masters stated.

"I didn't want to put too much on her," Jasper explained, frowning at him. "She's still staying at the hospital."

"Yeah, but this could be instrumental in finding out what happened to Mason."

Jasper rubbed his forehead as he thought about it. "Look. I'll talk to her again. She was doing a little bit of work, but she was getting so tired that I didn't want to add more."

"At least ask her," Masters suggested. "She won't appreciate being kept out of it, and she is somebody who wants to be involved. I get that we need to keep her safe, keep her *and* the baby healthy," he noted, "but mentally she would benefit from keeping busy and being included."

Jasper's lips twitched. "Maybe. I'm not so sure you're right though. The late term of her pregnancy has her drained, not to mention the worry about Mason."

"Maybe not," Masters conceded, "and I've been wrong before, but I also know what it's like to be kept out of the loop when it's important, when something you could do might make it go faster or even smoother—or whatever adjectives we want to use," he said, with a wave of his hand. "The wording doesn't matter. Just give her the option and see what she says."

"Will do," Jasper agreed. "Now, this file on Nicholas. For the moment, we don't know that any of this is related to Mason's case."

"But you're considering that it could be, right?" Masters asked.

"Honestly, I don't see how it *can't* be."

"Yeah, I get that there are likely to be multiple cases that Nicholas was involved in that could very well have impacted his disappearance," Masters shared. "However, for something happening to Mason so soon after a navy investigator goes missing, I think we must consider the potential for a connection. Am I saying it is connected? No. Am I saying it needs to be investigated? Hell, yes. So is anything coming together on Mason's shooting?"

Jasper winced. "Not in any positive or tangible way, no," he admitted. "We've tracked down all the city cameras following all the vehicles leaving the base airport at the relevant time. We've tracked down the one vehicle we have determined to be the getaway vehicle. It was stolen. We found no DNA in or on that vehicle, though forensics is still going over it all. So far, nobody is plying me with anything positive in that direction," he stated. "We both know how hard this investigation will be, since it appears to be a professional hit."

"A professional hit on a base full of professionals," Masters pointed out, "so definitely not an easy round of things to lock down."

"But not impossible because, in order for it to happen here, somebody here had to be involved to some degree."

"I agree with that," Masters stated, "which is also why I'm clearing everybody here, from snipers to supply clerks. And, of course, we can't let our personal feelings influence anything."

"You mean, *Sam*. No, we can't," Jasper agreed, with a directed look at the room outside of his office. Jasper went on. "Just because Sam doesn't appear to be a team player and is more than chafed that I appear to have some influence that he doesn't know anything about, all that doesn't make him a shitty person or guilty."

"No, it doesn't make him a shitty person, and neither does his sobriety struggle, but it does make him somebody that we can't necessarily put our trust in at the moment," Masters declared. "And we need all hands on deck for Mason's investigation."

"Exactly. I am heading off to look at ballistics today," Jasper shared. "I have a few questions for our ballistics team."

"About what?"

He gave him a look. "Apparently some anomalies were found in the bullet that they pulled out of Mason."

"Anomalies?" he questioned.

"Yes. And I'm not saying that these were custom-made, but I'm thinking more along the lines that they were homemade."

"Ballistics should have been able to tell you that already."

"Yes, they should have, and, in a way, I'm getting what feels like a coded message that it's quite possible. Still, I want to know why it's not a clear-cut deal. Thus I have a meeting scheduled with them," he explained, as he checked his watch, "in about an hour."

"Did they set it up?"

He nodded.

"So, they found something then," Masters stated, excitement in his tone.

"And yet they're calling me," Jasper pointed out.

"Right. Shit. So, we're back to the potential for trouble here in the department again."

"We're certainly back to something. I just don't know what. It's hard to figure out what's going on here, when you and I are so new here as it is," Jasper noted. "And there's obviously a lot of underplay happening."

"Yeah, plus we have a missing investigator, whom nobody appears to give a crap about finding, which is a huge red flag for us, and obviously for his family as well."

"I will keep you in the loop on this ballistics deal. Why don't you take the Nicholas angle and run with it and see if you can find anything? In the meantime, if I need you to do something with Mason's case, I'll tag you."

"Done." Masters stood and walked to the door of Jasper's office, then turned to look back at his boss. "We're both playing in the dark here, and you know how dangerous that is," he muttered, "so watch your back." And, with that, he turned and walked out.

CHAPTER 5

ELIZABETH WORKED FROM home for most of the morning, getting buried in client calls and accounts. It was almost 11:00 a.m. before she looked up and realized just how much time had gone by. She got up, stretched, walked over to the kitchen to put on the teakettle, and stared out at her backyard.

She and Nicholas had planned to get puppies together at one point, hoping that, if one of them was traveling, the other could look after both. Having such a system in place, they could enjoy the benefits of having animals, yet share some of the load when they each needed to be gone.

And yet it hadn't worked out quite that way. Her brother was gone more often than not, and she was home most of the time, and still they'd never quite got around to getting a pet. She could have had a puppy or a cat anytime, and yet something always made her hold off. Right now she could use the comfort of having a furry animal here on a constant basis.

She forced herself to not open the files that her brother had kept on that USB, wanting, maybe quite wrongly, to somehow double-check his peace of mind. Yet, if he were dead, that was completely foolish. However, the longer he was missing, the more that his death seemed to be a distinct possibility. She knew that's what the initial investigators had thought, both at the base as well as among the civilian cops she had spoken to. She also figured they assumed she had been involved in whatever had happened to her brother. They probably figured they would wait her out until the body was found, then pounce. After all, there was no statute of limitations on murder.

Elizabeth sighed.

As far as she was concerned, that was just a lazy excuse so neither the civilian nor the military investigators had to look any further. It was the easy way to fob off questions they didn't have answers for. She didn't know how to make that clear to anybody though, because nobody gave a crap about finding Nicholas, but she did. She wondered how many other people were caught in such an ineffective system, such an uncaring bureaucracy that claimed they were right and you were wrong, with no recourse when you had no proof, when you had nothing but that feeling that something seriously wrong was going on.

And when her brother didn't come back, and nobody believed her, she was stuck with no place to turn. The unexpected arrival of Masters had definitely brought hope back to Elizabeth again, though she knew it was dangerous. She'd gone down a spiral of never-ending torment to the point that she had nearly jeopardized her job because she hadn't been able to focus on anything but finding her brother. Only in the last month had she pulled back and given her job the attention it deserved.

Other people didn't have to pay the price for whatever had gone on in her brother's world, and thankfully Elizabeth still had the means to support herself. That her brother was worth a fortune, leaving her an incredible inheritance upon his death, didn't matter to her in the least. She would do anything to get him back. Just something about knowing she could be the last one left in a long line of family made her realize what was of value in life, and it had absolutely nothing to do with dollars and cents.

With a fresh cup of tea, she walked out to her front porch and sat down in her chair, just sitting in the sun, enjoying the moment. When she heard a woman call out, Elizabeth looked over to see her neighbor Dolly waving at her. Remembering what Masters had asked of her, Elizabeth got up and slowly wandered over to the older woman, hopefully in a casual and natural manner.

When she arrived at Dolly's porch, the woman patted the seat beside her. "It's nice that you've got your own cup of tea," she greeted her in delight, "because I have a cup too."

Elizabeth sat down on the big swing bench with the older woman and smiled at her. "How have you been lately?" she asked.

"Oh my, I'm fine," she replied, with a wave of her hand. "Obviously you aren't though."

"I'm doing better," Elizabeth muttered. "Time does help heal wounds."

"Oh, I'm sure it does. I'm sure it does," Dolly reiterated, with a gentle tap on Elizabeth's hand. "I'm so sorry for all the problems you've been through."

"Thank you." Elizabeth gave her neighbor a small smile.

"It seems that you have a new man in your life," Dolly announced brightly.

Inwardly Elizabeth groaned because, if anything caused comments in her world, it would always be about a new male. "He's just a friend," she compromised.

"And that is exactly what you need now," Dolly declared. "We all need friends in our difficult times."

"Isn't that the truth," she muttered. She looked over at her brother's house, easily seen from her spot on Dolly's porch.

"And no word on your brother, is there?" Dolly asked.

"No, not yet, but I keep hoping."

"And hope is what keeps us going day to day."

Hearing the same platitudes she heard from so many people all the time, Elizabeth smiled and nodded. Unless people had been through something like this, they couldn't understand just how painful and difficult this was.

"I did notice you over at your brother's house," Dolly added.

"I should be going over more often," Elizabeth shared. "There was a window open that I hadn't noticed. That's not something I want to happen."

"Oh dear," Dolly replied, looking at her with interest. "Were windows supposed to be open?"

She shrugged. "Unfortunately I don't remember. With my being over there so much, I tended to not notice."

"Yes, yes, that happens. And, of course, a couple service guys were over there," she pointed out. "They probably left it open."

Hearing her words, Elizabeth stiffened slightly and frowned. "I don't remember bringing in any service workers. Do you remember when that was?"

Dolly frowned and stared off in the distance, as if trying to remember when it was, but then she shrugged. "It wasn't this week," she muttered. "I can't be sure if it was last week either," she added apologetically, "but it wasn't too-too long ago."

"*Hmm.*" Elizabeth pondered that.

"Maybe you forgot to pay a bill for your brother," she suggested. "When you're dealing with so many things, I'm sure his bills aren't exactly at the top of your mind."

"No, that's true, and I certainly found a few that needed to be caught up," she admitted, "but I thought I got them all." She stared off at his house.

Dolly added, "I was quite surprised at just how long they were there."

"What does that mean, timewise?" Elizabeth asked in a wry tone, as she studied the older lady. "Was is ten or fifteen minutes, maybe thirty?"

"Oh no, they were there a couple hours."

Elizabeth stared at her in shock. "Really? And did they take anything away with them?"

Dolly looked confused for a moment. "I don't know. I didn't see them walking to their vehicle," she explained apologetically, "but I did see the van leave, and they were in a rush. It's like they just—"

"They?" Elizabeth stopped Dolly for a moment. "When you say *they*, are we talking more than two?"

"No, I saw two men," Dolly replied, "but I don't know how many may have come and gone. It's not as if I sat out here and watched them the whole time. If I had thought it was a problem, then I would have, but I didn't think of it as a problem back then."

"No, of course not, and any problems you noted would automatically be related to my brother's disappearance."

"That's the thing though. I didn't think about it," she admitted apologetically. "Now that you're asking me all these questions, I'm wondering why I didn't think about it at the time," she said, her voice rising.

"It's fine," Elizabeth replied, patting Dolly's hand. "It might have been the police. I don't know. They may have asked for clearance, and I thought they were coming in one day, and they came in on another day."

The other woman relaxed at that. "Oh. Oh yes, that would make so much more sense," she stated.

"Did you see anything on the vehicle itself?"

Dolly shook her head. "It was a white van. Like a delivery van. And I've seen the police use things like that on TV," she noted, "so I'm sure that must have been what it was."

The mention of TV as being a real-life representation of what was going on was a little much for Elizabeth to swallow, but she also knew that the older woman was just appeasing herself with it. "But you didn't see that they took anything with them?"

She shrugged. "I don't know. When I first saw them entering the house, they had little toolboxes," she shared, with a shrug.

"Right. And that makes sense, particularly if they were searching for something or setting up something," Elizabeth noted. "I'll ask them."

"Oh yes, do that," Dolly agreed. "After all, it's your brother's house. You should get the details of what they were up to," she declared, indignation making her voice rise.

She smiled at her. "Not to worry. I'll check it out. If you do see anybody else at the house, let me know, will you?"

"You mean, outside of that cute young man you had with you?" Dolly asked, a twinkle in her eyes, switching from one topic to the other, back to the whole romance thing.

"Something like that," Elizabeth replied, with an eye roll. "Not that I'm saying he's an important part of my world, by any means."

"Honey, he stayed at your house last night," Dolly exclaimed, with a nudge and a wink. "We already know that he's important."

Flushing at the immediate innuendo the other woman implied, Elizabeth realized just how little people could hide in some ways. Yet, in other ways, people could enter her brother's house and be there for hours, and nobody noticed. Her brother's house wasn't in a direct line of sight from Elizabeth's place, unless she stepped out onto her back deck. And sure, she did go out on her deck on an irregular occasion just to have a cup of tea and to enjoy the world, but it's not as if she sat there, tracking anybody coming and going, and that in itself was upsetting.

She stayed for a few more minutes and asked a couple more questions. Not getting anything helpful, she made her excuses and headed back to her place. As soon as she got inside, she phoned Masters. He answered on the first ring. "Wow, that was fast," she joked. "What were you doing, sitting on the phone?"

"Hey, maybe I was waiting for a call from you," he replied.

"I don't know why you would do that," she muttered. "My world is a mess."

"Did something else happen that made you worried about that mess?"

"I talked to my neighbor."

"Oh, good. What did Dolly have to say? Wait. I'm not that far away. I'll swing by, and we'll talk about it." Not giving her a chance to say yes or no, he ended the call.

She walked back to the front window, wondering just how far away he was. After all, he didn't mention whether he was twenty minutes away or ten. She hadn't had lunch yet, and now all she could think about was whether she was supposed to invite him to stay for lunch or completely ignore feeding him. She groaned at the etiquette of something like this, knowing that her grandmother, who'd been incredibly fastidious on that stuff, would have had a heyday just chastising her for even wondering.

Deciding that she would take the more hospitable route, and, if he didn't want anything, that was fine. She could have it tomorrow. So she quickly made up a couple Dagwood sandwiches. She was just putting it all together when she heard the knock on her door. She walked over and threw it open, a smile on her face, only to freeze as she stared at a delivery man, holding out an envelope.

"I'll need a signature, please," he said.

She looked down at it and replied, "I'm not expecting anything."

He shrugged. "I don't know anything about it. I'm just the delivery guy."

Realizing that he probably had no clue about anything, she quickly accepted the envelope and signed for it. Just as she went to close the door, Masters pulled up and parked on the other side of the street.

She waited until he approached and got inside, shutting the door behind him, before she shared, "I just got this envelope. I had to sign for it."

"Are you expecting anything?"

"No."

At that, he took the envelope from her and studied it more closely. "And it bothers you?"

"I'm not even sure that *bothers me* are the right words," she clarified, "but it's definitely not something that I was expecting."

"Right. In that case, let's take a closer look." He motioned her into the kitchen.

He slipped on a pair of gloves and carefully opened the top, and a single piece of notepad-size paper slipped out and fell to the ground. He bent down and picked it up, setting it on the counter. She appreciated the fact that he didn't even appear to be looking at who might have sent it. Resisting the urge to grab it, she gasped.

"What?" he asked, now reading the handwritten note out loud over her shoulder. "*Do not go to the police.*"

"Don't even ask me about this because I have no idea. Why would they even say that? After the investigators on base ignored me and my brother, I *did* go to the local police, but that was months ago. And they were of no help either." She turned to face Masters, frowning. "Unless they think you're the police."

"I'm military police, at least one form of it," he replied. "So maybe."

"And that would assume that they knew you were," she pointed out.

He smiled and nodded. "That's a very good assumption."

As she stared again at the note, she sensed something building inside her, realizing it was a flicker of hope. "Dear God," she exclaimed, "does this mean Nicholas is alive?"

"No, it does not mean that." When she glared at him, Masters shook his head. "It *could* mean something like that, but we don't know enough to make that leap."

"You're just stopping me from thinking that way."

"I'm stopping you from getting hurt," he clarified. "It's possible your brother is alive, and we've always known that could be possible. It's also possible that he's not and that he potentially has been deceased since day one. We don't know yet. I just don't want you getting your hopes up too high, not when he's already been missing this long."

Her shoulders sagged. "Even if he were alive, where would they have kept him, and why for many months?" she cried out.

"Exactly," Masters noted. "For them to do something like that, it would be a very long-term plan, and they must have had a reason to keep him alive for such a long time. I'm sorry. It just doesn't make sense."

"That doesn't mean it's not possible though, right?'

He took a deep breath and nodded. "Right, but we don't know that."

She winced, her mind furiously churning through all the information she knew. Why would somebody take her brother and keep him hostage? That was the thing she didn't understand. "If," she began, "and I know you'll say there are no *ifs* here, but, if Nicholas is alive, if they've been keeping him alive, what possible reason would there be for that?" she asked, turning to look at him directly.

"That's what we have to find out," he muttered. "However, this note changes everything."

"But does it, or is it just somebody playing games? Somebody tormenting me?"

He winced at that. "Do you live in a world where you have people who would know about all this and do that?"

She stared at him. "I don't think so, but the world we live in is full of people who do things like that for kicks."

"Unfortunately you're correct there," he muttered. "I'll get this over to forensics for their analysis and see if we can come up with anything on it."

When he turned to leave, she asked, "Are you coming

back?"

He nodded. "Yes, I'll be back. I just don't know when." With that, he was gone.

MASTERS WALKED INTO forensics with the hand-delivered letter, then quickly explained what the problem was, and asked if they could put a rush on it.

The tech behind the counter just stared at him.

He smiled. "And, yes, I can get you all the authority that you want." He pulled out his phone and quickly phoned Jasper. Having explained it on the way over, Jasper was waiting for his phone call. Masters handed his phone to the tech, and very quickly Jasper set out and put in place the hierarchy of who had the right to request what. It was a very minor department in the sense that most people didn't even know any lab and testing went on here at the base. Yet, as Coronado had ended up with several cases happening right here, the navy's investigation department had built up to the point that a lab on base had become a necessity, with the rest all contracted out. Luckily people were ready and available onsite. Masters handed off the note and wondered if he should just leave or what.

The lab tech noted, "You won't get a result very quickly."

"And when you say, *not very quickly*, what does that mean exactly?" he asked.

The tech hesitated. "I can work on it this afternoon, if it's important."

"It's important," Masters confirmed.

The guy winced but nodded. "Fine, go have lunch or

something." With that, he turned and walked into the back.

Not sure even what *lunch* would constitute in terms of a time frame, Masters stepped out of the lab, walked to a coffee shop across the way, ordered a coffee and a muffin and sat down, sending Elizabeth a quick apology. She responded with a similar text, saying it was fine, and she was just having a sandwich for lunch.

Then she phoned him. "Look. Instead of having your coffee and a snack," she offered, "come over here for a sandwich. I made them before you arrived, but then you took off so fast that I didn't have a chance to even tell you."

He hesitated, checked his watch, and then realized that he might as well. He changed his coffee to a to-go cup, headed for his vehicle, and pulled up in front of her place a few minutes later.

As she opened the door, she smiled. "I had literally just made sandwiches when you walked in the first time."

"Sounds good. If I'd realized it, I would have come right back."

She pointed to the kitchen table and said, "You might as well sit down. I've got everything ready."

When she brought over the sandwiches, which were big, he looked at them appreciatively. "When you say a sandwich, you meant a real sandwich."

"I do like my sandwiches," she shared, with a chuckle. "Most people today have no idea what a sandwich was meant to be. They put a little slice of ham and cheese between two pieces of bread and call it a sandwich," she explained. "That is not my idea of a sandwich at all."

He agreed and was grateful to have the moment to sit down and just take a time-out. He bit into the sandwich and realized it was quite worthy of taking a whole lot more than a time-out. He quickly polished off his first half and sighed with pleasure. She looked over at him, one eyebrow raised, and he nodded. "That's a very good sandwich."

She chuckled. "Thank you. So, how long do you have to wait for the forensics?"

And he realized he hadn't even brought her up-to-date. "I was able to put a rush on it, so I'm just waiting to hear."

"Good," she said. "The sooner we can get answers, the better."

"You just need to know that I probably won't say anything to you about the results, not until we get this solved."

She rolled her eyes at that and didn't say much, and he felt as if he had betrayed her trust. But he couldn't do a whole lot, not until he had a chance to examine everything else going on. She didn't say anything, just continued to munch. He finished off his sandwich and still had no phone call from the tech, so he knew it could end up being a whole lot longer.

"Had you seen that courier before?" he asked, deciding he might as well make good use of his time while he was here.

"No, and, no, I wasn't expecting him at all. I assumed it was you at the door," she shared. "It was a surprise to see him."

"You opened your door without looking through the window?" he asked, narrowing his gaze at her.

She paused, thought about it, and nodded. "Yeah, I sure did," she muttered. "That comes from that whole *living an innocent, blameless life* thing."

"Sure, except that now your brother is missing, so that *innocent, blameless life* is about to become not quite so innocent and blameless."

"And that sucks," she muttered.

"Sorry," he replied, his tone gentle. "It's just the facts of life."

"I know. I get it. I really do," she murmured. "Yet it's not exactly anything I want to deal with."

"From now on you need to be incredibly careful. This person, whoever sent that note, knows where you live, likely knows that I have been here, knows that your brother is missing—and potentially could have had something to do with his disappearance."

She stared at him for a long moment, the color leaving her face, as she nodded. "I was hoping to ignore all that."

"Ignoring this reality is something you do at your own peril," he declared. "Right now, your brother is missing. What we don't know is whether he's dead and what the possible reason could be. And you're in finance. I don't know how big your clients are. I don't know anything about it, but I'll need to."

She stared at him, slowly lowered the last bite of her sandwich, and nodded. "When I was initially dealing with my brother's disappearance, a bunch of my accounts switched to somebody else," she shared. "I didn't think anything of it because honestly I wasn't doing a very good job for my clients at that time. So I half expected that my client allocation would take a hit. Yet I figured I would get them back some day. One client hasn't been returned to me, though most of the others have. That one client is big," she muttered, "and from another country."

"You want to tell me what other country that is?"

She winced and whispered, "Colombia."

His eyebrows shot up. "So, what investing do you do?"

She shrugged. "The usual. I've been working with this

bank for a long time."

"And you've got no hesitation about working for them, nothing asked to be done under the table, nothing that would make you suspicious of any illegal activity? Nothing suspicious about this Colombia client itself?"

"No, not at all," she declared. "I started working for the bank's owner years ago. Then the owner's son, Fred, took over, maybe three years ago, but everything's been fine, and the transition was smooth. I still see the owner occasionally, but he's thoroughly enjoying his grandkids and his retirement."

"And the son?"

She shrugged. "Fred's not my kind of guy, but that doesn't make him bad," she shared, with an uncomfortable laugh.

"When you say, *not your kind of guy*, what does that mean?"

"It means he fools around, like in terms of office romances. He's cut a wide swathe through the females and has a tendency to change it up frequently."

"Never you though?" he asked, point-blank.

"No, never me," she stated, "and honestly I'm probably too old for him anyway. I'm thirty-two. He goes for the twenty-five-year-olds."

"So, he definitely doesn't want anybody seasoned and mature, who knows her own mind," he noted, with a laugh.

"Most guys don't," she declared, with a pointed look. "They all want somebody they can train into being that submissive wife."

"Not everybody," he corrected. "A lot of us prefer to have someone with spirit instead of blind obedience."

She nodded. "I'll take that into consideration the next

time I see one of these romances brewing around the office," she stated bluntly. "Honestly Fred's not the kind to give a crap whether she has brains or not either. Trust me that he's looking more at cup size."

"That's because he hasn't grown up yet either," Masters pointed out, with a chuckle. "Not those women's fault. It's probably … I don't know why those office romances happen with Fred, but I presume it's the thrill of it."

"Probably," she muttered. "Not my scene, but it is one of the reasons I'm happy to work from home."

"So, you don't see a lot of what goes on at the office?"

"I see a lot. I just don't see everything, now that I work from home full-time. So, I'm definitely out of the loop to some degree."

"And this one client that you didn't get back, is that a concern for you?"

"Not really," she replied. "I think it may have been for the best anyway. He wasn't exactly my … I didn't get along that great with him. He was old money, and we always must be very polite and considerate and all that jazz," she shared. "Yet some guys don't think women belong in the workforce, especially when handling finances, and he always wanted a man to deal with his money," she shared, with a note of self-mockery.

"Of course. I guess you probably get a lot of that."

"Finance is still considered very much as a man's world," she murmured. "And most of the time I don't give a crap at all. I just do my work, and I'm good at what I do. And I don't make waves. Making waves makes life difficult, and I'm not into difficult. Right now, I just want solutions for my brother."

He smiled and nodded. "Understood."

"You find my brother," she added, "and the whole world, my world, will completely change."

"What if they're not the answers you want?"

She winced. "Obviously I want him found alive, and every day that passes makes the chances of that seem even slimmer and less possible," she murmured. "But hope? Hope is everlasting, and I just—I need that hope."

"Of course," Masters agreed.

She stared at him. "You come from a very different point of view, don't you?"

"No, not at all," he countered. "I agree that hope is everything, but I also know that, way too often, we can have as much hope as we want, and still the results are negative."

"That's your history speaking," she replied, "and it's probably why it makes you a good investigator. From my perspective that is something I don't even want to contemplate. But I appreciate that you will be that influence of reality and experience, while I will be the hopeful optimist."

He laughed. "Being an optimist is a good thing, particularly when your brother's life is hanging in the balance. If he is alive, we also must consider the fact that he would have been kept as a prisoner somewhere, likely not in the most wonderful of places."

She stared at him and nodded. "And that's very disturbing."

"It is," he agreed, "not only disturbing, but he'll probably need medical attention and therapy."

"I don't care about that. I'll sell my house or whatever it takes to get him back on track."

"Seems your brother has enough money to do that on his own."

"Yes, he probably does." She remembered that and

brightened. "I contacted one of the companies that he invested in, a dot-com investment into a friend's venture, and they've known each other since grade school. My brother gave him the start-up money, and he had a 50 percent share. So, when the company got big enough, they bought some of his stock to give the guy more of an ownership share, and that's where some of Nicholas's millions came from."

"Good," Masters stated, knowing this was a huge plus. "That is very helpful and will keep our train of thought away from something criminal going on."

"It's not illegal money. That's what I was concerned about too," she shared.

"Of course, and you were right to wonder when that much money is involved."

"But you also know that, when it comes to some of these investments, it can be big money, massive money," she pointed out. "And honestly it's been huge confirming that Nicholas's investment had netted him such a wonderful return on investment. And his friend did know that my brother was missing and told me that my brother still has a bunch of shares in the company, which would all probably come to me in the event of my brother's passing. He asked if I have any idea what I wanted to do with it. I told him in no uncertain terms that I just wanted to focus on getting my brother home, which, as you can imagine, created an awkward moment. Then we talked a bit more, and I basically just ended the call."

"Did you feel any sense of relief on his part that you didn't want to do anything with Nicholas's remaining shares?"

"I don't think legally I can do anything unless we find a

body," she shared. "And I don't think … I think he was hoping that I was correct to hold out hope, back-pedaling a bit, making it sound as if I wasn't loopy for holding out hope when he's been missing for so long. However, for me, there will always be hope."

"I think every family member feels that way," Masters noted. "And people who aren't in this position don't understand."

When his phone rang just a few minutes later, she jumped.

He held up a hand and said, "It's just the lab. It's all right."

CHAPTER 6

ELIZABETH SANK BACK down and listened, as Masters answered his phone. She didn't know why she was so jumpy, but that courier at her door had changed everything for her. Yet it also made it seem a lot more possible that her brother was alive. All she could think about now was that she'd missed something. Had there been something that had gone on all this time that she hadn't seen and sorted out?

Masters had been right when he suggested that, from now on, she would have to exercise more caution. Assuming it was Masters at her door and flinging it open without a thought was foolhardy. While she had thought it was Masters, she also realized it was more than that. Another part of her still raced to the door to see if her brother was coming home.

She waited for Masters to finish his phone call, and, when he got up, she realized that this visit—or whatever it was—was officially over. She watched as he continued his phone conversation on the way to the front door. There he ended the call and told her, "I've got to go, sorry."

She waved him off. "Tell me what you can, when you can, please."

He stopped and nodded. "That is a reasonable request.

Thank you." And, with that, he was gone.

She stayed at the front door and watched as he drove away, feeling an odd sense of loss, something she hadn't expected. She didn't know whether it was because he was the first person who seemed to give a crap about her brother's disappearance, or because of who he was and the fact that he'd been looking out for her, and had come when she phoned.

So many things were mixed up in her head, and she didn't want to confuse emotions for something completely different. She liked Masters very much. He was a good man and seemed to care. He was a breath of fresh air when it came to all the other investigators she had dealt with on this case. It had seemed as if nobody had given a crap, and the fact that her brother was part of their own team had been forgotten.

Elizabeth was pretty sure that Nicholas would be heart-broken to think that nobody had considered his disappearance important enough to truly investigate, and the fact that they thought she may have had something to do with it was also devastating.

She understood why it would be considered, but she couldn't imagine it would have been all that difficult to clear her, if they had only wanted to. Harming her brother, the only person she had in the world, was something she wouldn't and couldn't ever do. Nicholas was an important part of her life, and no way would she ever do something to hurt him.

She thought about her own finances, wondering if she would need to free up some money, just in case. If a ransom was suggested, she would pay it in a heartbeat, but she would also have to liquidate some of her assets to do so.

With that in mind, she quickly cleaned up the kitchen first, putting on tea next, and headed back to her computer, then settled in to return to work. Yet, in the back of her mind, she was looking at her options, figuring out what she could do if she was called to do something.

Frowning, she went through some of the investments she held jointly with her brother. She'd convinced him early on to invest in a few things, and she did control those in the sense of being his adviser on them. She checked his account, and everything there looked normal and stable. It was the one account that hadn't been taken away from her when she had been struggling over her brother's loss. Her lack of attention to her accounts had not gone unnoticed.

Now she was doing much better, or at least she thought she was. When her supervisor phoned her a little bit later and asked her to step into a group meeting, she stepped in virtually and listened, as the new CEO ranted about some new restrictions and some changes in the company policy.

Her eyebrows shot up as he talked about making people return to work in the bank, and she realized just how that would impact her day. Normally she worked from home and went in sometimes. Up until now, that had been fine. However, the new CEO was talking about making everybody come back in, and with positive attitudes. She kept her face schooled, watching other people's reactions, noting a couple of them not liking it at all, including her immediate supervisor.

When it was over, her supervisor phoned her, and he asked, "What do you think?"

"I think it sucks," Elizabeth replied. "I come in when I need to, but I certainly don't need to be physically in the bank all the time to do my job."

"And you're still hoping for changes with your brother's situation, of course."

"Sure, of course I am," she replied, "but that has nothing to do with my work."

He hesitated.

"Wait. I've been back on track and making work a priority."

"Yes, and it was at least partly my fault for not taking away some of that work earlier. Once I realized what was going on, I should have removed some of those accounts from the get-go, so that's on me."

She was surprised to hear him say that, but he'd always been a very fair supervisor, and she appreciated the fact that, when she hadn't been able to look out for herself, he had been there.

"I guess there's been no news on your brother, has there?" he asked.

"Actually there might be now," she muttered. "I just don't know which way it'll all go."

"Oh? … That's huge, isn't it?"

"Maybe. It's nothing's so huge, not when it's been this many months."

"Right," he replied, his tone deepening. "I'm sorry about all this."

"Me too, and I certainly don't need more issues at work, but I'll deal with it."

"So you'll work at the bank now?" he asked.

"The new rule doesn't take place for a while. Maybe the lot of us will boycott it, and the CEO will change his mind," Elizabeth suggested, not even believing her own words.

Her supervisor asked, "Or will you … quit?"

"Quit? No, I wasn't looking to quit," she replied. "Is

somebody saying I am?"

"No, I'm just getting an idea of what's going on," he explained. "Nobody seems to be particularly happy."

"Nobody likes change," she pointed out. "We can get quite comfy in our own space, and there's no real reason for us not to work from home."

"I know. I understand," he said, "and we start work early."

"You guys do. I'm not on a stock market bench, like you guys are, so I work a bit later."

"Right, another point in your favor," he noted. "Anyway I'll see how everybody reacts."

"Will you challenge the CEO over it?" she asked, with a note of amusement. "Or will you consider quitting?"

"I'm considering it," he admitted. "Yes, it might be a good time."

"Right," she muttered. "And this new CEO, being a friend of Fred's and all, is that how this works?"

"Yeah, they're friends, and apparently he's been monitoring our work-from-home situation for a while now, and suddenly he's decided that we all need to come back in," he shared, with a note of humor. "I assume he's spoken to Fred and his dad about it, but I don't know that."

"I don't think any of this will apply to Fred anyway, so he probably doesn't give a crap. As long as it keeps the money flowing and the business moving in the right direction, he won't care either way. Interesting tactic though. He may lose a bunch of people."

"I know, and that's what I'm sorting out, like just how many will bail," her supervisor told her. "It's hard enough to get people now anyway, especially qualified people. No matter what, it'll be painful."

"And that will be on your plate too, I suppose."

"Somewhat, yes. Depends on how many people leave from the various departments and whether I leave too," he replied. "Anyway, have a good rest of your day." And, with that, he was gone.

She stared down at her phone, just wondering about life, and its ability to send you for a loop out of the blue. The last thing she needed right now was something like this, but that was also one of the reasons why stuff like this happened.

With a shrug, she settled back in and buckled down to tackle the rest of her workday. She had just finished up when her phone rang. She looked down at it and didn't recognize the number, but that wasn't an oddity in her line of work. She often felt she needed to answer phone calls that were not numbers she knew, and so she did. Nobody replied on the other end, and she went to hang up, when a faint voice finally spoke.

"Sis?"

She froze.

"Sis, help me." With that, the phone went dead.

MASTERS WAS JUST walking into the forensic lab to talk to the technician when his phone rang. He looked down, saw who was calling and frowned, but he answered it. "Hey, I don't have any answers yet, and as I—"

"No, no, no," she cried out. "I just got a phone call." She gasped, her breathing hard, clearly rattled.

"Easy, easy, calm down," he said. "Who called you?"

"My brother," she cried out, with joy, tears, and pain all reflected in her tone.

"What do you mean, your brother?"

"He said, *Sis, help me*, I can't believe it."

Masters ran his hand through his hair, as he turned and walked back out of the lab, so the conversation was private. "Did he tell you where he was?"

"No, no," she cried out in hysterics. "The line went dead at that point."

"Crap," he muttered.

"I know. I know. He's alive. He's alive! Don't you understand what this means?"

"I understand some of what it could mean," he replied cautiously.

Suddenly she caught on that he didn't see this as good news. "I don't understand why you're not overwhelmed with joy," she responded. "I am."

"I would just like to know for sure that it was your brother."

"Oh," she muttered, and dead silence came afterward.

He winced. "Look. It's the world I live in. I don't want to kill your joy, but let's just make sure that somebody isn't playing you."

"Right," she said, her tone more formal but in control.

"I don't suppose you have a number for that call."

"I checked right away, but it was a private number," she explained, "and it didn't, ... it didn't tell me anything."

"I'm at the forensics lab. Let me talk to them. Then I'll get right back to you." He quickly hung up, walked back into the lab, and asked the techs at the counter, "If you have a recent phone call on a cell, is there any way to track it?'

They instantly frowned. One spoke up. "If it's a private number, not really, but, if something else, maybe we can deal with it forensically."

"Meaning what?"

"Just that we might get a location from where the call came from."

"It read Private Number, but she has no record of it beyond just that the call came through."

"Right. So, therefore, it was probably fast and short, leaving no way to trace it."

"Right, that's what I was afraid of." Masters sighed. "So … back to the note. What did you guys find?"

"Not a whole lot," he began. "No fingerprints were on any of it, the note or the envelope—other than Elizabeth's. We also don't have any record of this writing anywhere in the database," he added. "So really, we don't have anything. I'm sorry. We were hoping for better news."

"Me too." He thanked them, then turned and walked back out, calling Elizabeth back. "Did you recognize his voice?"

"I don't … I don't know for sure," she told him, her tone subdued. "It was barely above a whisper and happened so fast."

"I'm sorry," Masters said. "I don't want to stop the hope here."

"No, but you're right. If it was Nicholas, why wouldn't they have contacted me a lot earlier? If it isn't him, who the hell is playing these games?" she snapped, anger at being played coming through quite clearly.

"We also have to acknowledge the possibility that it was him and that he found a way to get a call out."

"In which case," she noted painfully, "chances are, he's paying for that indiscretion."

"Unless the kidnappers set it up," Masters noted. After another long silence, he added, "I've just come out of the forensics office, and unfortunately nothing was on that note or the envelope, no fingerprints other than yours, which was to be expected."

"Hey, wait, when you mean, *mine*? … Oh, right."

He smiled. "You'd forgotten that they fingerprinted you to clear you of anything."

"At the time I wondered if they fingerprinted me to find me guilty," she murmured.

"You still believe that, don't you?"

"Can we trace a call?" she asked.

"No," he said. "They weren't on long enough, and it was a private number, so it's probably a burner phone that they've already tossed by now."

"But what would be the point of that?"

"That's the question," he muttered. "Does anybody want you to go off the deep end? Does anybody want you to quit? Does anybody want you to do anything in your world that something like this would stir up?" She sucked in her breath, and he winced. "I gather there's a yes in there somewhere."

"I … I don't know," she replied. "Let me think about it. I'll call you back." And, with that, she was gone.

He stared down at his phone in frustration. She hadn't done anything wrong. She'd done only what he had done to her, which was abruptly end the call. Still, it was frustrating that she had something in the back of her mind but wasn't willing to share it just yet. He drove back to the office, and, as he walked in, he heard a heated discussion ahead of him. As soon as he showed up, the conversation stopped. He looked inquiringly from Sam to Morgan. "Problems?"

Sam snorted. "As if you should have any part of this."

"Am I the problem?" Masters asked with a smile, as he

noted Sam's disgruntled look.

"We don't know anything about you."

"No, and you might want to consider if that's why I've been brought in."

At that, both men froze, their eyes widening.

"What?" Sam muttered.

"Think about it. One of your own team members disappeared, a case not solved, and now we have another major event on this base," he pointed out. "Also a case not solved. And who knows what other issues we have in this very department."

"Hey, Mason's case just happened," Sam protested. "And we're all on it, but we're not getting very far."

"Maybe that's part of the problem too," Masters noted. "The fact that the situation with Nicholas was never resolved is also a concern."

Sam snorted at that. "We were told not to waste too much time on it because they were pretty damn certain who was responsible. The fact that you seem to be all over this chick is a whole different story."

At that, Masters frowned and faced them. "Did you investigate her? Did you clear her or find anything to convict her? Did you do anything other than take insinuations from the brass as real? Do you have any reason, logic, or evidence to prove it?"

"No, of course not. If we did, we would have arrested her."

"So, you did nothing, and, when she finally went to the local cops and her lawyers, it pissed you guys off."

"Sure, she made it seem that we were at fault, but we weren't. We'd been doing everything we could."

"Did anybody keep in touch with her, let her know what

was going on?"

"It's not as if we have a customer relations department," Morgan said, finally speaking up. "Keep that in mind too."

"Sure, I get that, but she felt she had no choice but to bring in lawyers because the entire military organization had stonewalled her."

At that, Morgan winced. "For an outsider I'm sure it felt like that."

"Absolutely it felt like that, and, if you think I'm sleeping with her or in some way compromising my position," Masters spelled out, noting Sam's immediate eye roll, "you can put that right out of your head."

"Right? As if we're supposed to believe you," Sam muttered.

"I don't give a crap whether *you* do or not," Masters replied, "but I will not tolerate disrespect. So one of us needs to go right now, and you choose which," he added in a cool tone.

Sam stood in shock.

"Yeah, I'm serious. This isn't how any military department works, and this isn't how an investigation into the disappearance of a member of this military force should be treated. This isn't how Nicholas deserves to be treated. I don't know what shit's going on down here," Masters added, "but I sure as hell don't want anything to do with it. If you guys are compromised because of it, I will find out." And, with that, he turned and walked into Jasper's office.

Jasper stared at him as he came in.

"I presume you heard that."

"I deliberately make sure I hear everything that's going on," Jasper stated. "Definitely no love is lost on those two, yet I don't know why."

"I don't know why either."

Jasper nodded. "They sure don't like any comments about Nicholas though, do they?"

"Not only that but they're 100 percent against his sister, which I find odd. I don't know about you, but, so far, I haven't seen anything that points to her being involved."

"I haven't either, but I also know that there's been some file tampering."

At that, Masters raised his eyebrows, as he turned to stare at Jasper. "Are you serious?"

Jasper nodded. "Quite a bit is missing here. No statement from her as to where she was at the time. A whole lot of information I would expect to have is not here, something that would at least show a thorough investigation had been conducted. Instead what I'm left with is a skeleton of an investigation, which will make these guys look bad if they're ever called to account over it."

"Why would they do that?" Masters asked, puzzled. Then he frowned and asked, "Or is somebody else doing it?"

"That's the question."

Masters opened the door and called out to Morgan. Moments later Morgan stepped in, but it was obvious he was still pissed off from the earlier exchange with Masters.

"Close the door, please," Jasper ordered.

Morgan stiffened but closed the door and turned to face him, his arms crossed.

"The investigation file on Nicholas's disappearance," Jasper began, "contains no statements documenting you guys have interviewed Elizabeth in any way."

"Sam and I both did," Morgan claimed. "All of it's in the file."

He spoke with such an off-handedness that Masters got

pissed off all over again. "Are you always this sloppy and lazy with your investigations?"

Jasper snapped at Morgan, before he said more. "Look at me."

At that, Morgan turned and stared at him.

"I am telling you that no interviews or statements are in this file involving the sister, about the sister, from the sister, at any point in time." When Morgan started to bristle, Jasper stopped him again and went on. "I don't think you understand what I'm saying here. This file, as it stands right now, shows that you guys haven't done jack shit to find your colleague. Now I don't know whether that's how you want this to go down or you want to believe that we somehow removed material out of this file, but take note that the computer system absolutely does not allow us to have access for deleting things like that. So you might want to consider just what's going on here. Either you guys completely dropped the ball on this case or somebody wants you to look as if you never did squat, if it ever comes to a full investigation."

Comprehension slid across Morgan's face. He sat down with a hard *thump* on the seat next to Masters.

Morgan whispered, "What the hell?"

CHAPTER 7

ELIZABETH PACED THROUGH the main floor of her house, going from the kitchen to the living room and back out to the kitchen, her arms clamped around her chest, as she assessed whether anybody at her job could have sent her a phony call from her brother. The fact that the CEO wanted to enact these new return-to-work rulings might have made her missing brother now calling her somewhat more of an issue. Yet surely they would have just fired her, rather than pulling a stunt like having a fake recording of Nicholas show up now, enticing her to quit rather easily. She ended up talking herself into a good case against her boss, Fred, and his new CEO, but then right back out again because she had absolutely zero issues with her direct supervisor. Besides, this new *return to work* maxim surely affected everyone at the bank, so why would it be done simply to single her out?

When Masters called a little bit later, she greeted him by saying, "I'm sorry. I didn't mean to hang up on you earlier."

"Of course you did," he noted, in a wry tone. "We're having a bunch of fun here too."

"Good," she said, "hopefully it's productive fun."

"Not really," he admitted. "How about you? Anything pop to mind?"

"Lots, and I think I've talked myself out of all of it."

After a moment of silence, he suggested, "It might help to talk things over with somebody else."

"And that's true. It might be helpful, but it also might be a great disservice to people."

"It's not as if I'll turn around and arrest people if there isn't any proof that they've done anything wrong," he pointed out.

She loved the dry humor that came through so clearly. He had such an expressive voice, and his face? ... She'd heard that phrase about having a very emotionless face, versus somebody who showed every expression. She'd always thought that she was expressive, but Masters took the cake when it came to that. "No, you're right," she admitted. Then she hesitated and asked, "How about coffee?"

"At your place?" he asked.

"Yeah, I didn't even get a chance to tell you about what Dolly told me," she muttered.

"What was that?"

"Apparently two *workmen* were at my brother's house a couple weeks or so ago," she replied.

"Workmen? Did you assign them?"

"No, I didn't know anything about it. They came through one day, and Dolly said that, when they left—some two hours later—they left in a big hurry."

"Damn."

"I suggested to her that maybe it was the police and that they got called away on another case, and she was all in agreement that that was quite possible because she'd seen that happen on TV." Elizabeth let a laugh escape. It was either a laugh or a cry because she sure couldn't keep track of her emotions right now. She was all over the place.

"Yeah, don't we love how TV portrays things like that," Masters muttered.

"She couldn't identify them, only that it was a white unmarked van. Two men, white van, and toolboxes. And she didn't know about anything else," she muttered. "And she didn't remember what day it was, only that it wasn't last week and she thinks it might have been the week before."

"And she never thought to mention it to you."

"No, she sure didn't, at least not until I asked her about it. Then she was hoping that maybe it might have been the police going in to check things because she didn't want to think that she had missed something."

"No. Most people are generally good to help out," he noted. "And they're not looking to cause us harm. They generally just get by and have a good life themselves."

"Right. I would have said that Dolly was in that category. She's always been there, capable for the most part, friendly, and she's the one who often keeps track of what happens around here."

"Which it seems she did again in this case, kind of."

"She did, indeed," Elizabeth agreed. "It's just a little confusing as to what these people would have been doing in the house."

"Looking for the USB key perhaps."

"Have you been through it yet?" she asked.

"Not all of it, no. I haven't had two seconds."

"Right."

"So, do you want to tell me what else is going on?"

She winced and muttered, "Not really."

"If you had to hang up on me to consider all the ramifications of something—presumably to do with your job," he began, "it would be nice if you would fill me in so that I can at least be down the same pathway."

She groaned. "Now we're back to that coffee thing."

"How about I take you out for dinner instead?" he offered.

She stared down at the phone. "Are you allowed to do that?"

"Meaning?"

"Meaning what?" she asked. "I'm a suspect in the case, after all."

"Yeah, that's one of the things I wanted to talk to you about."

"Oh, do you have a reason to bring me in?" she asked. "I think I would consider that a betrayal if you're only being friendly to get answers."

"I'm not being friendly to get answers. If I wanted answers, I would haul you down here and get the answers the way I would with any suspect," he explained. "However, I don't consider you a suspect, and I don't know exactly what's going on with you, but I do have a couple more questions I would appreciate some answers to."

"Great. So, am I supposed to come down to the station?"

"No, that's why I asked you out for dinner," he stated. "You suggested coffee, but it's almost dinnertime—in case you hadn't noticed."

"Oh, good Lord," she muttered, staring at her phone in shock. "I hadn't even noticed that."

"I understand. And the problem is, we've got an awful lot going on right now, and we're not exactly paying attention to what could be some interesting developments. The fact that two men were at your brother's house is very important, and I'll get techs on that right away."

"And what can techs do?" she asked.

"They can look for street cameras to see a white van leaving your brother's place, maybe find out where they went and what they were up to."

"Oh my, then I guess it would have helped if Dolly had mentioned something earlier, wouldn't it?"

"Yes, it would have. We would certainly have had more notice to get information on it."

"But that would also have implied that somebody gave a crap."

"I'll tell you this once and for all. I care, and I give a crap," he declared. "I'll figure this out. I'll come and pick you up in about twenty minutes, so be ready." And, with that, he disconnected.

CHAPTER 8

ELIZABETH DRESSED QUICKLY, changing from her shorts into jeans and grabbing a lightweight T-shirt and a sweater. She locked up the front door, stepped out onto her front porch, and waited for Masters to show up. True to his word, he was right on time. She walked down to meet him, instead of his getting out and all, and also waving at Dolly, who sat on her front porch.

Dolly smiled and waved back.

Masters looked over at Dolly. "She's got a bird's-eye view of your house and Nicholas's, doesn't she?"

"She does," Elizabeth noted hesitantly. "I do worry if she's in danger though."

"Hard to say. It depends on whether she's got anything that she's hiding—or she will give information freely to anyone who comes and asks her questions," he replied, his tone way too serious for her liking.

"That won't make me feel any better," she muttered.

He glanced over at her, as he pulled out into traffic. "Was I supposed to make you feel better?"

She groaned and muttered, "It would be nice."

"A lot of things in life would be nice," he replied. "And, right now, I need to hear more about that phone call."

"Nothing much to say. I got the phone call in this raspy voice, which did sound like my brother. He said, *Sis? Sis, help me*, and then the call ended," she shared, shivering at the reminder. Typical of Masters, he caught note of her shiver.

He asked, "And you believed it, didn't you?"

"I did, yes," she admitted. "But I don't know if it's because I wanted to believe he is alive so desperately." He smiled at her, and such approval filled his expression that she sighed and shared, "I'm not completely gullible."

"No, but you love your brother, and you want him home. That makes you vulnerable, not gullible. So, don't confuse the two." He continued. "But being vulnerable makes you an easy target because what you want is something other people can exploit. And that brings us back to what came to mind when I asked you whether anything may or may not have been a trigger for getting you to quit—or something along that line."

"When you said *quit*, something came to mind. We had an online meeting today, where they're ordering all of us back to work at the bank, even though most of us have it laid out in our contracts that we can work from home. I go in once a week at least, and, up until now, that's worked just fine."

"And this is coming from Fred, the son of the man who you started working for."

"Probably, but it came from the mouth of his new CEO. Fred has hired a friend of his to be the CEO, so that Fred doesn't have to work quite so much," she shared.

"And the new CEO's pushing this."

"Yes. So, then my boss, my actual supervisor, called me after the meeting, where we were informed of the new terms, and he asked me how I felt about them and was I likely to quit."

At the word *quit*, he glanced in her direction.

She nodded. "It just seemed out of character."

Silence came for a moment.

She added, "And yet they could have just fired me, instead of forcing me to work from the bank each day. There is absolutely nothing stopping them from doing that, outside of the fact that they don't have any cause," she noted, with a laugh. "But, during the time that I was first dealing with my brother's disappearance, I was in trouble and had too many clients to maintain. My supervisor did take the blame for that, saying that it was his fault and that he should have relieved me of my caseload.

"But they're *clients*, not just numbers to us. These are people we work with intimately and have done so for many years. So, it's not somebody you just pass on. In many cases, even after understanding what my situation was, several wanted to stay with me. I think that caused some ill will within the bank. However, if it had been anybody else, honestly I think it would have still been the same thing.

"You develop a relationship, and when you develop a good working relationship, then you stay with that person, and you hope that everything in their world rights itself, and it'll all be fine. In my case I won't say it's all fine because my world obviously isn't fine. Yet, I think, from a client's point of view, it did right itself. And, although I didn't get all my clients back, I did get the bulk of them. For the ones who didn't leave, nothing changed," she added, with a shrug.

"But if the CEO or Fred wanted to get rid of me, don't kid yourself. There are one million ways to move someone on without too much trouble," she stated. "So it doesn't make any sense that they would order everyone to return to the bank to work there, hoping that I alone would quit. If they were hoping I might quit, that might be a different story, thinking that I'm already on edge, and that something like this would send me right off again."

"But what would be the point of that?" he asked, looking at her directly.

"I don't know. I've been sitting here thinking about that, figuring out just why, and it doesn't make any sense."

He pulled up in front of a family restaurant.

She looked at it and smiled. "I haven't been here in a very long time."

"Neither have I," he said. "It just seemed to be the right place for tonight. Come on. Let's get some food. Both of us are running on empty."

"We had sandwiches not that long ago."

"*I'm* running on empty anyway," he clarified, with a laugh, as he snagged her arm and tugged her toward the restaurant. "Let's go. We need to eat."

"What happens if you're seen out with me? Will you get in trouble?"

He shook his head and muttered, "No, it doesn't work that way."

"Are you sure?" she asked. "I'm pretty damn certain we were followed."

He nodded and whispered, "I agree, and that's another reason I want to get you inside that restaurant."

MASTERS QUICKLY GOT Elizabeth inside and texted Jasper. He was looking as the vehicle went past slowly.

"I don't know what you can see of the license plate," she

whispered at his side, "but all I got was two letters, an *L* and a *J*."

He nodded. "And I got two more," he muttered. "So, between us we're doing good."

"If you say so," she muttered, as the vehicle tore off down the road. "I presume at the end there they saw us now watching them."

"Hard to say," Masters conceded, "but the fact that we have picked up a tail is fascinating."

She frowned. "You call that fascinating?"

"I do," he said, with a smile, touching her on the cheek. "It's okay."

"It doesn't feel very okay," she muttered.

A waitress hurried toward them, apologizing for having left them standing here.

But he smiled at her and replied, "It's all good." Then he nudged Elizabeth forward to follow the waitress.

When they were seated, he looked around at the location of the table and nodded approvingly. The waitress asked them about drinks and menus, and he told her they wanted menus, then looked over at Elizabeth about the drink question.

She shook her head. "I think I would like a clear head."

He raised an eyebrow but didn't argue, and the waitress returned with just water. As they went through the menu, he felt the waves of stress coming off her. Finally he put down the menu and shared, "It could have just been from an altercation I had at work myself."

Her eyebrows shot up. "You mean, they've finally figured out that you have some power?"

"No, they haven't figured that out yet at all," he declared, "but they're pushing it. So they'll soon figure out just where Jasper and I are at, and they won't like any of the answers. Also we're beginning to wonder if some people in the department aren't playing against each other."

"I think that's what people do," she stated bluntly. "Sometimes I wonder if they do anything but play stupid games."

He nodded just as the waitress returned and asked them, "Are you ready to order?"

He looked down at the menu he'd partially seen and asked, "What's the best burger you've got?"

She launched into an explanation, and he stopped her halfway. "I'll take that one."

She wrote it down, then turned to Elizabeth, who ordered a green mixed salad with chicken.

As soon as the woman was gone again, Elizabeth leaned forward and noted, "We have too many suspects."

"We do, and yet I think the bottom line will be that phone call."

"Sure, but how do we know where it came from? It was very quick, with few words, and yet I swear to God it was Nicholas."

"It's the *I swear to God it's him* part that I find fascinating because, in order for somebody to make it seem like it's your brother, they must have a copy of his voice." He watched as she sat back. "And all kinds of things can be done to video and audio these days. So, if somebody does have a recording of his voice, it would not be hard to edit the tape to say what you wanted it to say. And, yes, we have seen similar things before," he added. "And I'm sorry to say that. The other alternative," he said, as he took a deep breath, "is that your brother is alive."

CHAPTER 9

"I VOTE FOR the last one," Elizabeth stated. "I heard his voice. *His* voice. I heard the panic in it. Even if somebody else had a copy of his voice, I don't think they would have been able to make it sound *that* real. I'm just sorry he couldn't tell me something, anything that would have helped find him. Then, if he got caught making that call, of course he probably got punished in a way I don't even want to contemplate."

"Right, but the risk was obviously worth it to him, so the question is, *What's going on and how?* But you can certainly believe that we're all on this."

"All of you?" she asked. "I don't think those investigators in that office give one crap about what happens to my brother," she declared harshly. "I saw how they felt about it."

"Are you aware that, as far as they're concerned, this was you murdering your brother?"

"Sure, I told you that."

"But how did they get that idea about the money? That's what I don't understand. There's no proof and nothing to show you had knowledge of his investments four months ago, right?"

She frowned, but nodded.

Masters continued. "You received absolutely no financial gain here, not without a body, so where are they getting this theory from?"

She stopped and stared, then shook her head. "I have no idea. How am I supposed to know where they got this theory or what locked their brains onto such a stupid idea?" she cried out. "And, if somebody did that on purpose, why?" He waited for the answer to filter in for her. Elizabeth stared at him, then snorted. "Because then they were off the hook."

He nodded. "Exactly."

She let out a harsh breath. "Do you think that's what happened?"

"I don't know," he admitted. "I'm meeting Jasper later tonight. He's talking to a few people, some other cohorts who may potentially have some information. Plus we have asked somebody, who has clearance way the hell above us, to do some research that the others in the department won't like."

"Why wouldn't they?"

He winced, then leaned forward and whispered, "Because it's Mason's wife."

"And he was just shot on base?" she asked cautiously.

He nodded. "Yes. And she's heavily pregnant."

She winced at that. "God, what she must be going through right now."

"It's agonizing, terrifying really, but she's willing to do absolutely anything she can to help solve this."

"Of course she is," Elizabeth declared, "just as I am for my brother. It doesn't matter what anybody says. We know in our heart of hearts that something's wrong, and they're still alive. But something's up, and I don't care what it is," she snapped. "You just need to find Nicholas. I'm damn sure that was my brother's *live* voice was on that call, not just a copy."

He nodded. "And I believe that you believe that. I'm willing to go with it, but you must understand that the phone call itself wasn't terribly helpful, beyond the fact that it'll now trigger renewed interest in the investigation."

"But that's a good thing, isn't it?" she asked.

"Yes," he agreed, smiling at her. "It's very good, but …"

She sat back and stared at him, wondering how there could be a *but* in something that was so good.

Masters asked, "Why would somebody do that? Why would somebody trigger interest in an investigation that had basically been let slide into a cold case, one to be solved somewhere down the road?"

She blinked at him. "I don't know, but presumably because they want … They want something."

"They want something," he repeated, with a nod. "But what is it that they want, and why do they think they can get it by utilizing your brother? Honestly I see absolutely no reason to keep your brother alive all this time if he wasn't worth something. And, if he is worth something, just what is it that he's worth?"

Elizabeth stared at him, reaching for the glass of water in front of her and taking a long, slow drink, as she tried to assimilate his questions.

He leaned forward and whispered, "I know this isn't anything you want to be thinking about, and nothing is normal about this in your world, but this *was* your brother's world."

She blinked again at that and then nodded slowly. "Yes, that I will agree with. It was his world, and he loved it," she said. "So, the next question is whether anything in his world might have triggered this, but I don't know that," she admitted. "I would have thought that his teammates should be answering that question."

"And I would have thought that as well," Masters agreed. "Do you know his teammates or anything about them? Can you think of any reason why they may not have done a full investigation into this?"

She shook her head. "You mean, like, did he have a problem with any of them?"

"Yes. Did he have a problem? Did he ever say anything about them? Did he have an unkind word to say or to tell you about any problems he had with them? Did he get a negative review or—"

"Wait, wait, wait. I get it. I get the idea." She sipped on her water, as she thought about everything he'd just asked. To even think that somebody Nicholas had worked alongside of, somebody he had endured the inevitable daily successes and failures with, that somebody he should have been able to trust to have his back, would have had anything to do with this just made her sick.

"Don't think about anything other than this one focus," Masters stated. "Is there somebody in his world—work or personal—who might have had a reason for him to disappear like this?"

She shook her head at that. "If there was, it has to be related to the work that he did, which I'm not privy to," she pointed out. "It has to be on your end. It has to be something that you can find out."

"And I will. I will," he stated. "However, it would save us an awful lot of time and effort if we had a single direction to go in."

"Right," she noted. "I didn't even think of that. Once

again we have too many options, don't we?"

"Absolutely. We have them coming out of the wood-work," he stated, with a smirk, "and not necessarily in a good way."

She nodded. "Do I get time to think about it?"

"Yeah. You have to the end of dinner to think about it. After that, well, I'll head back to the office and start tearing apart the investigators' lives."

She winced and nodded. "Okay, let me see if I can think of anything, but Nicholas didn't talk shop with me."

"The bottom line is, *What would be the benefit of keeping your brother, A, alive and, B, away from everything in his world, including work, personal life, and home?*"

"And did you look at that Evidence file of his in relationship to his disappearance?"

"Yes, but this is what I'm thinking about right now, while we eat. Then I'll go back to the office and meet with Jasper. We'll start pulling on our additional resources because that phone call, … that phone call, whether it was meant to trigger a new investigation or to trigger a psychosis on your part, it has changed everything."

CHAPTER 10

ELIZABETH DID AS Masters had asked and considered what she could possibly know that would point him in the direction he needed to go, to narrow down the suspects. When dinner was over, Masters again asked her for suspects, and she shrugged. "I've got nothing. As far as I'm concerned, it's got to be connected to that USB key."

"It does make the most sense," he noted, "but we're still very short of information on it."

"But you see something on it, right?"

"Yes, we've got people digging into the USB file. So far we found information on a case, a case that was not investigated by his office."

She frowned, as she stared at him. "Was there any information on it?" she asked. "Did Nicholas even have the clearance or whatever to be looking into that case?" she asked.

"Not necessarily. We don't know that yet. I haven't been able to access the individual files, as Nicholas encrypted them. So we've got people working on recovering whatever information is on it."

She nodded. "Do you think it was a case my brother was looking into privately?"

"That's possible," Masters replied. "Again I don't have that information yet."

"And would you tell me if you did?"

He nodded. "If I can, yes. I don't have a problem sharing that information, unless it's classified at a level that would make that inappropriate, such as, top secret," he added, with an eye roll.

"Isn't it all top secret? Aren't you guys all crazy about the status of information such as that?"

"To a certain extent, sure," he agreed, "but you should be kept in the loop to a certain extent as well."

"I don't think your coworkers believe in that," she muttered.

He smiled. "Right now, my boss is Jasper, and Jasper has a very different outlook on how we treat the family of the victims." She winced at the term, and he nodded. "The thing is, that's exactly what you are, and whether Nicholas is alive or not doesn't change the fact that he's a victim of a crime and that you are his family."

"Do you think anybody but you will move on this case now?"

"They are certainly taking a hard look, at least Jasper is," he said, correcting himself.

She stared at him. "Why do I get the feeling a big cover-up is involved?" He gave her a flat stare, and she groaned. "So, sharing the truth with the family will only go so far."

"Exactly. Those conversations only go so far. I don't have tangible information, so you'll have to leave that part of it until I do."

She hesitated, wondering if it was safe to trust him, when his phone rang.

He answered it and held up a finger to her and whispered, "Hang on a minute." He put a hand over the mouthpiece and said, "I need to take this call privately. I'll be right outside." And, with that, he quickly walked out the front door, talking on his phone.

As she sat here and waited, the waitress came around and asked her if she wanted coffee. She hesitated, not sure what Masters would want, then decided what the hell. She could use a cup regardless. She ordered coffee for them both. When he returned to the table a few minutes later, his expression was a lot less approachable than before. She groaned. "So, that doesn't look like good news."

He gave her a quick glance. "Did your brother ever say anything about a Gary Trojan?"

Her eyebrows shot up, and she frowned. "I've heard that name, something to do with his work, I think. I'm pretty sure. Why?"

"Something was in the Evidence file. I'm to ask you whether Nicholas ever talked to you about it."

She slowly shook her head. "If he did, it wasn't much. It wouldn't have been a *Sit down, this is important, and we need to discuss this* conversation or I would remember it," she explained, looking at him. Then she rubbed her forehead, closing her eyes.

"What is it?" he asked, as she was obviously getting something.

"I think maybe that Gary Trojan had some connection to somebody who worked at the bank." She stared off into space, then pulled out her phone and brought up the directory on the bank's website. She turned her phone so he could see. "This guy, Larry Trojan," she said, tapping the picture on the screen. "According to this, he still works there, but this directory hasn't been updated in a while, and I don't think he's there anymore."

"Do you know what happened?" he asked, staring at the name and the face in the photo on the bank's website.

"I'm pretty sure he was let go for some reason," she replied.

He sat back, his fingers rapping on the tabletop in front of her. "That's pretty interesting."

"It's a connection that I hadn't considered," she shared, staring down at the phone.

"Did you have anything to do with him?"

She shook her head. "No, I didn't, but the new owner"—she frowned—"Fred might be friends with him."

"Might be? Define friends?"

"I don't know for sure," she noted. "I just remember seeing them together at one point in time, laughing, like they were old friends, but I guess in a work scenario you don't ever know what that means."

"True enough," he muttered. "Okay, so leave that to me. I'll do a history on both and see what we can come up with."

"Does this come back down to me again, then?"

"I don't know that it comes back to anybody," he noted, "but information about *Gary* Trojan was on the USB key."

"Right. So, there's a chance my brother might have found out something about somebody who works with me."

"It's possible, yes."

"But then, why not use that information to get me to do something?"

He hesitated, then said, "This is a good time for me to ask you point-blank if anybody has asked you to do something because of Gary or Nicholas. Has that happened in any way?"

She stared at him in shock, then glared at him. "No,"

she snapped, "and if anybody had pressured me to do something illegal or unethical, I would have gone to the police." His smile was one of the gentlest she had ever seen on a man's face.

He nodded. "You love your brother, and you would do anything to save him."

Tears came to her eyes, as she covered her face and nodded. "Yes, that is true. I would have theoretically done anything I could to save him. But I haven't had any such request or any communication with Gary or Larry Trojan or about Gary or Larry Trojan."

"Would anybody else at work have access to your emails or have access to anything in your office area that could have compromised your emails?"

"Sure," she said. "I don't even answer most of my own emails. We have a computer system that sends certain emails regarding certain topics or certain clients to various designated people at the bank. Then we have a person at the end of the day who sorts through the ones that don't go anywhere else. Obviously I use my email for my private clients, and when I say *private*, I don't mean outside of the bank, but *private* as in clients I've worked with exclusively for a very long time."

He pondered that. "So, to the best of your knowledge, no way could any email directed to you have been ignored or deleted or diverted elsewhere, like outside of the bank's personnel?"

"No," she replied. "To the best of my knowledge, that's true. And if you are telling me now that somebody has been waiting for a response, that makes no sense, not after so many months."

He nodded absentmindedly, as he stared out the window.

She studied his face, wondering what new horror was emerging. "It would help if you could tell me what else is going on."

Jolted out of his thoughts, he turned to her. "The thing is, I don't know what else is going on. After I take you home, I need to meet up with Jasper," he reminded her. "Hopefully, by then, they will have gone through more documentation on that USB, and we may have a better idea of what is happening."

"Will you even be allowed to tell me?"

"I don't know. I will talk to them and see."

The waitress brought the coffee just then, and Elizabeth looked down at it and muttered, "Somehow I don't even want this anymore."

"We ordered it, so let's sit and enjoy it," he suggested. "I didn't want to upset you, but these are questions that have to be asked."

"And yet you asked a variation of them already."

"I did, and this case just got a little more convoluted, I guess."

She groaned. "It still doesn't explain why Nicholas has been held captive as long as it's been. If somebody did have my brother and if they planned to utilize him to blackmail me into doing something, that would have nothing to do with Mason's case. That would have been a blackmail scenario addressed to me some four months ago. And I can't see a way to explain why they held off all this time."

"It's the *holding off* that I don't understand either," he muttered. "It's got to be some timing issue."

"So, that would imply that something threw off their timing because there's no need to kidnap Nicholas months ago only to hold off doing anything with that leverage."

"Unless he was about to do something, and, by kidnapping him, they prevented it."

"But not killing him?" she asked, raising her eyebrows.

"I don't know," he muttered. "We still lack some critical information."

She smiled. "Maybe. But I have to say that whatever intel you do have, I am not at all upset to hear that people are considering that Nicholas might still be alive."

He gazed at her intently and nodded. "You do realize that if he is alive, he—"

"It doesn't matter. We'll get through it. Whatever it is that he's been through, we'll figure it out. We need him home so he can heal," she explained. "He's strong. He's capable, and I know that whatever has gone wrong in his world happened because he found out something that other people didn't like."

"You have that much faith in him?" Masters asked.

"Absolutely. I know him inside and out," she declared. "Nicholas is one of the good guys in the world."

"We need to get him home, … if he's still alive. And I sincerely hope that he is."

MASTERS WAITED UNTIL Elizabeth finished her coffee, then to see if she was ready to go. She stood up and nodded. "Are you okay to go home alone?" he murmured.

She nodded again. "Absolutely. You go figure out whatever the hell is going on. That's more important."

"No, it's not. It's also important for you to stay safe because, no matter what's going on, somebody was at your brother's place."

She winced that. "And it was a professional-looking deal," she murmured.

"Meaning that they rented a van and had uniforms."

She nodded and winced again. "Of course that's pretty easy to imitate, isn't it?"

"Unfortunately, it's all too easy to imitate. Two guys, overalls, toolboxes, heading into an empty house. Yeah, way too easy."

As they got into the car, she asked, "Any chance they put bugs in his house?"

"I've been considering that," he replied. "I know where there's a bug finder. I might borrow it and take a run by Nicholas's house."

"Let me know if you do, please."

"Oh, don't worry. I'll be coming to check out your place as well."

She stared at him, shocked, and then sagged back into the seat and closed her eyes. "God, going down this pathway is not what I expected."

"It never is," he stated. "But the farther down this pathway we get, the more we find out, and it's likely to get uglier before it gets better."

She rolled her eyes at that. "You could have at least told me that it would all be fine and that we would get all the information and that I would be having Sunday brunch with my brother before I knew it."

"Considering the fact that he's been gone for four months and that you haven't heard a word from him in all that time, it would be incredibly wrong of me to even imply such a thing. We don't know whether he's alive or dead. All we know is that somebody is playing games. I know that you believe he's alive, and we will hope for that. If they call you back, please contact me. Don't give them any information, and don't let them know that you're alone or that you contacted the police or anything else."

"No, I won't," she murmured. "At the same time, that's not exactly an easy thing to do."

"You could just not answer your phone," he suggested. "Just let it ring and see if they leave a message. For all they know, you're in the shower."

"Oh, that's a good point," she muttered. "As much as I want them to call, now you've made it so I don't want that call at all."

He smiled. "I'm not trying to set you off here. All I'm doing is asking you to keep all avenues open and to not get anybody into such a panic that they do something stupid."

She winced. "Ouch, that felt like it was directed at me."

"It's not," he declared. "Kidnappers, if they've opened the door to communication, can be extremely unstable."

"*Great*," she whispered under her breath. She got out at her house and added, "So, you need to be careful too."

He flashed her a bright smile and nodded. "Not an issue. I'll call you when I'm out of my meeting."

She hesitated, then he raised one eyebrow. "That's fine," she noted, with a shrug, then turned and resolutely strode up her front walk.

He frowned, knowing that coming back here wasn't the smartest idea. Yet something about that stiff back of Elizabeth's and the firmness of her attitude kept her spine upright. He called out to her and asked, "Is it okay if I come by afterward instead of calling?"

She flashed a bright smile as she nodded. "That would be great." And, with that, she ran up to her front porch.

He waited until she was locked inside, then headed down to his meetup with Jasper. As he walked into Jasper's office, he found Jasper angrily ending a phone call, glaring at the phone. "Looks like that went well," Masters said, as he turned to close the office door.

"No, it sure didn't," Jasper confirmed. "At the moment, my lovely boss doesn't want me to step on any toes, until we have more information."

"Which could make sense, depending on what a headache we're facing."

"So, this Trojan person," Jasper began, "was on the base and was convicted of smuggling on his way back from overseas. He always protested his innocence and declared it wasn't him, how it had nothing to do with him. He was eventually jailed and got quite badly beaten in prison. When he went to the prison infirmary, he somehow had a medical emergency and died. The USB key appears to have information that shows he was basically stonewalled into this."

Masters frowned. "So, Nicholas found information that another case had been fixed, so that this guy was charged and went to jail, and now that Nicholas came up with that evidence, it looks possible that somebody might have done the same to him?"

"That's one avenue of thought, and another one is here," he stated. "His office was told to park the case and to put it to bed. That it was a done deal and they needed to move on because they had other open cases to work."

"Moving on because you have other cases isn't necessarily a foreign thing, assuming the Trojan case was solved."

"And it was solved," Jasper replied. "Solved as much as anybody could deal with at the time. He'd already been in prison, and he'd applied for an appeal. This office was never asked to get any more information or to deal with it in any other way."

"Okay, so in that scenario, it's got nothing to do with this initial team then?" He had to smile at the amount of potential relief he was anticipating.

"But there are also signs that some of the documentation in this case had been presented earlier, giving him a full alibi. That alibi apparently went missing, and, according to the prosecutor, that documentation was never received on his side, and he's blaming this office."

"And does the information Nicholas had change that?"

Jasper rubbed his face, clearly frustrated. "The files on that USB key include the document giving Gary Trojan a full alibi."

"Okay, so I don't understand."

"Nobody does at this point, which is why I'm not allowed to bring it up any further. But it appears that Nicholas was investigating a case where Gary Trojan died in prison, after being convicted of a crime he didn't commit. Nicholas had found proof, some proof anyway, that the accused couldn't have done the job because he wasn't even in the country."

"That's a pretty big alibi to not have released," Masters muttered, exhaling.

"Exactly. Apparently some of his travel documents couldn't be produced at the time. Anyway let's just say that, for reasons we don't yet know the details of, everything went sideways, and this Gary Trojan guy ended up being convicted and then died in prison, never having had the chance to get anybody to believe his story."

"I wonder if he approached Nicholas directly."

"I don't know," Jasper replied.

As Masters sat down, he added, "So, here is another twist for you. This person who died while wrongly convicted … had a brother, Larry Trojan, who worked at the same bank as Elizabeth."

At that, Jasper sat back and stared at him. "What? You're kidding."

"She didn't remember where she knew the name from, when I asked her if *Gary Trojan* was familiar to her, but it wasn't long before she'd connected this *Larry* Trojan guy to her work, who has since been let go. And speaking of work, she also thought that something was weighing on Nicholas related to his work, though she didn't know any details. Anyway, back to the Trojan last name, she did recognize the name and brought up an employee directory from the bank's website." He quickly tapped on his phone and waited for the website to come up. "She was sure he'd been let go, but the website apparently hasn't been updated in some time, so his name and photo are still here on the bank employee roster."

He handed his phone to Jasper, who then opened the file on the desk in front of him, and brought up a photo of the other man's face. He showed both, side by side, to Masters.

"Definitely brothers," Masters muttered, as he compared the two photos.

"The question is, does that affect anything?" Jasper asked.

"I don't know," Masters admitted, "but it could be why the original investigation team was suspicious of Elizabeth's involvement in Nicholas's disappearance."

"Or worried about Elizabeth's connection to both Trojan and Nicholas." Jasper frowned at that and then nodded. "We obviously have some overlaps here."

"And we know that, in this business, overlaps are dangerous."

"Yeah, they sure are," he muttered.

"Also Elizabeth got a very short Private Number call from who she swears is her brother, which gives her hope he is still alive and seemingly nudges his case to be reopened." He looked over at Jasper. "But none of this so far applies to what happened to Mason."

"No, it doesn't. I did talk to Tesla, and she is looking into the lives of the four men who work here on this original investigation team. Technically, one of them, Steve, already on medical leave, was on his last active day the very first day I got here. He doesn't work here anymore."

"Convenient timing."

"I did wonder about that, and I do have Tesla finding out just why he's no longer working here."

"And, so far, nothing's come up on the others?"

"No, not so far. Tesla will do a bang-up job of finding their background info, but she'll also be slightly limited because she can only check records and search for any information that might tag somebody as being in a compromised position. We must be careful about going too far and getting into a scenario where either they or the brass gets tipped off. Which, if anybody knows that they're being watched …"

"Exactly," Masters interrupted. "Which reminds me of two more things. I texted you that Elizabeth and I were followed on our way to dinner. I've got one of Mason's team searching for that. We only got four letters of the license plate, but it's a start. And I want to borrow your bug finder and take a look at both Nicholas' house and Elizabeth's."

Jasper got up, pulled it out of the closet, and handed it

to him. "Let me know what you find on both those issues."

"Oh, I will. I'm still quite perturbed about this other case, the Trojan guy, because it seems we have somebody in this office potentially compromising cases."

"And that's possible, but it could also be somebody in the Records Office or somebody in the DA's office," Jasper noted. "We can't necessarily land any of that blame on this office."

"But the fact that Nicholas himself has potentially been resurrected as a kidnapping case, instead of a missing person's case, surely brings the point into further focus."

"Which is why the conversation I just had now has me so frustrated," Jasper stated, glaring at the phone. "The boss here is the same boss who the initial investigation team had talked to about making sure these cases were minimized. And not only minimized," he added, "but that the files are more or less hidden to the point that we had to ask for Morgan to get us access to the rest of the file."

They both nodded at that.

Masters noted, "It's still not getting us anywhere though. We have a dead, possibly wrongly convicted Gary Trojan, and we possibly have a missing investigator in Nicholas, and none of this currently connects to Elizabeth's job, to Elizabeth herself, or to Mason."

"I know," Jasper muttered in frustration. "And, of course, every time I talk to the brass, all they're concerned about is Mason."

"Of course, because the rest of this stuff has been in play for a long time, and nobody gives a crap."

"Maybe they do care, but it's all been in play for a long time, so, in their minds, a little bit longer isn't going make any difference because nobody has managed to break open any useful information yet. When there's no break in the case, you move on to the next one, and, of course, the next case right now is Mason."

"Any change in his condition?" Masters asked.

Jasper looked up and smiled. "The doctors seem positive. They reduced the sedation and brought him back out for some tests, then sent him back under again. I don't understand why or how, but apparently they're feeling positive, so we're going with that."

"That's great news," Masters murmured.

"It is, but it's not good enough because, as soon as he's awake, there will be holy hell to pay if we haven't caught whoever is behind this."

Masters laughed at that. "And that's something you'll be taking a direct hit on."

"Yeah, I sure will," Jasper conceded, with a grin. "Yet I can't wait because it will mean Mason's back to the world as we all know him. In the meantime, he's in a medically induced coma, healing enough to make his way back."

"So, where do we go from here?" he asked.

Jasper looked at the bug finder in Masters's hand. "Go deal with that first, and let's see if there's any reason to be concerned. If somebody is bugging Nicholas's house or Elizabeth's, that means they expect something to happen. One more thing. There is a rumor about drugs. And Gary Trojan."

With that, Masters raised one eyebrow.

"Yes, I did say drugs," Jasper confirmed, "and the only reason that would become an issue now—"

Masters nodded. "Is if the drugs might have surfaced or if somebody is making a move to get them. But why keep Nicholas all this time?"

"I'm not sure," Jasper shared. "Did you come up with any theories as to this four-month time frame?"

"The only thing I could come up with is that something changed in the time line. Maybe Nicolas decided to come forward with his suspicions, maybe somebody else was pushing him, or maybe … When was the death of Gary Trojan, this innocent man who died in prison?"

Jasper opened the file again. "He died a week before Nicholas went missing."

Masters nodded at that. "I bet that was the trigger. Whatever Nicholas was working on, maybe it became a moot point when the innocent guy died in prison, or maybe that's what made Nicholas angry enough to take the evidence he had and to push it forward. Maybe he pushed it to the wrong person."

"All of this is just conjecture," Jasper pointed out.

"Sure, but that time frame of the week Gary died and Nicholas went missing gives credence to that conjecture."

"In a way it does," Jasper admitted. "If Nicholas was pushing forward with this found alibi, angry that this young man had lost his life before Nicholas had the chance to do something to save him, somebody must have found out. So, they could have just taken him out with one kill shot. Why keep Nicholas for four months? Maybe they weren't ready for whatever they still needed to do, and they might still need Nicholas to make it happen, so they kept him as a backup plan."

"Four months is a long time for a backup plan."

They looked at each other, both knowing how rough being held prisoner for an extended time could be.

Jasper nodded. "It's a very long time. And it makes no sense, unless it ends up in a big payout, and the only reason in this case that we have so far would be the drug angle."

"And that would also imply that these drugs are connected to the military," Masters pointed out.

Jasper winced at that. "Which is bad news on its own, especially if it's connected to Mason's shooting."

"How would it be connected to Mason?" Masters asked.

"I don't know, but a part of me says it is connected somehow."

"Only if Mason found out something or if somebody had accidentally told him something. Could it involve that Arctic mission he'd just come back from?" Masters asked, sitting back and staring at Jasper. "Didn't the base up there have a drug problem?"

Jasper grimaced, as he sighed. "Among other things."

Masters nodded. "Then maybe they're worried that Mason had info while he was up there that would have jeopardized everything here. So, if they take out Mason and put Nicholas on ice, securing the mission yet again, who would care? Who would know?"

"That's a little bit beyond anything we would have considered normally," Jasper noted.

"These cases do appear to be completely unrelated, don't they?" Masters agreed. "And, if they are unrelated, we have absolutely no way to connect them because there *won't* be a connection. However, if there *is* a connection …"

Jasper nodded. "We have to consider the options. So, if there is a connection, we'll find it, and we'll make sure whoever did this pays. But we also must confirm that whatever is going on stops here at Coronado. It stops here. We can't let it go on and lead to more nightmarishly connected cases that nobody even knows about."

"If we're on the right track," Masters began, "one of the

clever aspects of this whole mess is the fact that nobody suspected any of this was connected, until—"

"Until we found that USB key that Nicholas stashed," Jasper replied.

"What are the chances that the two *workmen* seen a couple weeks ago at Nicholas's house were looking for the USB?"

"It's possible. It's very possible, but why didn't they find it?" Jasper asked.

"I don't know. Elizabeth found it at the very bottom of Nicholas's closet, under a slab of plywood put on the carpet to hold his shoes. That seems like it would have been a reasonable place to stash it, and yet easily found too."

Jasper looked at the key and frowned. "But look at this. It doesn't look like the usual USB key."

They both stared at what seemed to be a decorative keychain fob, shaped like a piñata.

"And is that something that Elizabeth might have given Nicholas?" Jasper asked.

"I thought she mentioned how she was the homebody, with Nicholas doing a lot of traveling. So seems he would have bought it for her, yet he kept it so maybe he wanted it for himself?" Masters shrugged. "I could ask her. She didn't seem surprised when she saw it, but it could just as easily be something he thought she might recognize."

"And that makes perfect sense," Jasper noted. "He could be leaving clues for his sister. So, ask her, take a photo of it just so that she has it to jog her memory, and maybe ask her that question when you see her tonight."

"How did you know I was seeing her tonight?" Masters asked, his eyebrows lifting.

Jasper smirked. "Who's the investigator here?"

"Both of us," Masters said, with a laugh. "However, you're right. I am going back up there tonight. Particularly after she got the phone call, supposedly from her brother. And I still want to check both houses," he added, pointing to the bug detector Jasper had given him.

"That phone call is another issue entirely," Jasper stated. "We could quite possibly be dealing with a hostage situation, and that means they want something and seem to think we have it."

"We found encrypted data on the USB. Any chance any of the material on that key is otherwise embedded? Like with steganography?"

"Pictures within pictures? Or words hidden within pixels?" Jasper asked, as he looked down at it and shrugged. "I have no idea. That would be one reason that they're still after it. Who would be our best bet in getting help with this on the sly?" They looked at each other, both realizing the irony of that question. Jasper nodded, with a sigh. "Tesla. Okay, don't worry. I'll bring Tesla into this too." He gave Masters a hard look. "Until we know more about what's going on, you best keep a close eye on Elizabeth."

"Oh, I plan on it." Masters checked his watch, then hopped up. "Matter of fact, I think I'll head back over there right now."

"Good. Stay close, at least until we know for sure what we're dealing with."

"I'm on it." And, with that, he walked out to his vehicle and headed to Elizabeth's house.

When he arrived, no lights were on. Frowning, he pulled out his phone and quickly sent her a text, asking if she was still up. When no answer came, his instincts kicked in, and he shut off the headlights and slipped around to the back of the house, worried that something was seriously wrong. As he approached from the back, still no lights were on. Going to the back door, he pressed his ear close against it and heard voices.

"If we don't take him out now, this will never end."

"This will never end anyway," Elizabeth snapped. "I don't know what the hell you're talking about, but this? *This* is past being a game."

"You're damn right it's past being a game," the man roared. "If it wasn't for bitches like you, it would have been over a long time ago."

Then came a sound that sent icy shivers down his spine—the sound of a single gunshot.

CHAPTER 11

ELIZABETH HOPED TO God that Masters didn't come back. Yet she couldn't stop thinking that maybe, just maybe, he was her light at the end of this tunnel, and whoever the hell was doing this would be stopped. Then she remember that scary assed gunshot. She glared at the two men in front of her, both with hoods over their heads so she couldn't identify them. She didn't recognize their voices either. So far, they hadn't said anything, except to ask her when Masters would return.

Since she had no answer for them, she hadn't been able to tell them anything. They'd made fun of her, telling her that she couldn't be much of a lay if he didn't even give her a time for when he came back for the next round. She just glared at them, refusing to react to their nasty innuendos. They were just hoping to get a rise out of her, and she wouldn't let them succeed. She didn't know what the hell was going on, but obviously something had taken a turn.

In a moment of daring, she asked, "Do you have my brother?"

The two men looked at each other, then started to laugh. She winced, knowing that this wouldn't be the way to get any information that she could trust. She sagged back in her chair, stared at the window, willing Masters to just arrive and not get in touch with her ahead of time. She didn't want to give these guys any warning. And yet, as she listened to them talk, antsy and upset that their prey hadn't arrived yet, she realized this was quite likely a hired job.

They didn't seem to know a whole lot except that they were to pick up Masters. The fact that they were after Masters at all amazed her. What could he possibly have that they wanted? Unless it had to do with the USB key he had walked away with, and anybody surveilling her brother's home would have known that. She never even considered that somebody had been in there. She'd been so adamant that her brother's place had been untouched, looking precisely the way it had when she last left it.

Her two intruders had been in her house waiting for her, throwing a hood over her head and subduing her instantly after she'd arrived home. Eventually they had removed the hood, making it easier to hit her. She'd been sitting here ever since, desperately in need of a bathroom trip, yet pretty sure it was only because of the panic she felt. And they just sat here, waiting for Masters to return. The fact that he was planning on returning at all had terrified her because that meant he would walk into this mess without warning. She had no way to tip him off, and these guys were just too rough, too ready, and didn't appear to give a damn.

"Where the hell is he?" snapped one of the guys. He turned and glared at her and, without warning, smacked her hard across the face once more. Her head snapped back, and she saw stars for several minutes, instantly crying out in pain. She'd tried so hard to not even let them know that she was rattled. Yet the more they hit her, the more she knew that she could not withstand much more. She desperately wanted to be that person who could, but she was sure that, if they sent any more beatings her way, she would give in.

And yet she had nothing to offer them; that was the thing that got her. She had absolutely no information. She didn't know when Masters was coming back, or if he even was. Just because she thought he was didn't mean it would work out that way. She didn't know what his schedule even looked like. So, here she was, captured by these assholes. Just thinking about how easily they'd taken her made her furious all over again. She slowly straightened her head and glared at them.

The guy who hit her scoffed. "You think you're so damn tough." He took a step toward her, but his partner held him back.

"If you beat her up too much, Masters will take one look at her, and he'll never help us."

The other guy snorted. "He'll never help anyway. We'll have to kill the bastard. This won't end up any other way."

The other man got a look in his eye, as if murder wasn't necessarily his first wish for this job. Too bad she couldn't see the rest of his face.

She glared at the one who kept hitting her. "That's all life is to you, absolutely nothing?"

"It's only money," snapped the first man. His voice was gravelly, as if he'd been a lifelong chain smoker.

The other one, a small rat-size guy, added, "No, we're not murdering anybody."

But Gravelly turned to him with mocking laughter. "Just because you don't want to doesn't mean that's not the way it will end up. I told them that right from the beginning. So don't go getting scared balls now."

Rat gave a nervous laugh. "That wasn't part of the deal."

"I don't give a shit whether it was part of the deal or not. This is a job. We do the job. We get more jobs," he snapped, "and then we have a decent life. Without the work, we got nothing. We talked about this."

"Sure, but you're not allowed to sit here and beat everybody up and kill them just because," Rat replied, as if pacifying his friend, who didn't appear to have any interest in being pacified.

"Why not?" Gravelly asked, as he looked back over at her. "It would make me feel better. I'm tired of waiting for this asshole."

"Tired of it or not, beating her up won't do anything but make our life harder, not easier."

"That's the only reason I'm holding off," Gravelly explained in disgust, as he looked over at Rat. "You and I both know that, if the bosses were here, none of this would happen."

"If the bosses were here, we wouldn't be in this position, and we would most likely both be dead," Rat pointed out.

That seemed to subdue Gravelly for a while, and then he just shrugged it off. He walked around, paced for a bit, and then flung himself onto one of the kitchen chairs hard enough that it rocked in place. Obviously this waiting was something he didn't like to do. When a racket came outside, he bolted to his feet and raced to the back door, but no other commotion was heard. He looked over at Rat.

Rat shrugged. "Probably the local dogs getting into the garbage can. I told you that we should have brought the garbage can in. At least then we don't have to worry about things like that."

"Go bring it in then," Gravelly snapped.

Rat laughed. "I ain't going out there. You just want to

use me as decoy, so you can take out this guy."

"I need to knock him out first," Gravelly muttered. "Everybody says he's wily, though I don't know how anybody even knows him."

"His service record. All that information is everywhere," Rat stated, with a smirk. "We would be foolish to ignore it."

Gravelly stared at his partner in disbelief. "Seriously? We've ignored so much other information on this job that we shouldn't have, right from the beginning."

"Whatever," Rat said. "Not a big deal."

And the garbage cans rattled again.

"Goddammit," Gravelly snapped. He walked to the back door, peered out the window, and shook his head. "Nobody's out there."

"Of course not, and, besides, if this Masters guy is coming, what are the chances that he'll just walk right in? No lights are on. Nothing says she's even here or still up."

"They told us to keep the lights off, remember?"

"Sure, but doesn't that tell him that something is wrong?"

"No, you idiot. It probably tells him that she's in bed, waiting for him," he replied, with a sneer, as he turned around to face Rat. "Although why he would want her, I don't know."

Sitting here listening to the insults flying back and forth, with Gravelly hitting her occasionally, was an odd experience. It seemed these two guys did this all the time, yet they had no care or concern about the effects on anybody else. They were completely focused on themselves. She wanted to say something, wanted to sneer at them or to insult them. She knew that would only end badly, and she was already dealing with a pretty rough headache from the blows she had taken so far.

She knew that Masters would be beyond furious when he saw her and realized they'd been using her for a punching bag. He didn't think very much of women being attacked. When she stopped and thought about it, she didn't even know how she knew that or why she was assuming that to be true, but it felt right. It felt like something he would be upset about. If he found somebody beaten up by assholes, Masters wouldn't hesitate to take some revenge.

That's exactly what part of her hoped he would do, while another part of her hoped he would stay away and not get involved. Yet still another part of her hoped he would get his ass in here damn fast and get her the hell out of here. If anybody could do it, it would be him.

She shuffled back in her seat, then closed her eyes. The blow came out of nowhere. She cried out in pain, her eyes stinging with the hard tears and sweat. She wasn't even sure where the sweat was coming from, but such a strong odor came with it. She looked up at Gravelly, who was glaring at her.

"If we can't sleep, you can't sleep. You close your eyes again, I'll smack you again."

She didn't say anything. She sniffled back the tears, as she tried to hold in the panic, wondering just how she was supposed to get out of this. Nothing she did was right, and everything she did seemed to set off Gravelly.

He turned suddenly and glared at her. "And stop sniffling. I can't stand snifflers."

She sucked in her breath several times, trying hard to stop the tears threatening to overwhelm her.

"Just leave her alone," Rat said. "The more you hassle them, the worse off they are. And the more they go to pieces."

"I know that," Gravelly spat. "I just—it would be nice if women wouldn't be such pieces of shit."

She stared at him in shock. How many women had they done this to, and why the hell should he be upset or surprised at women being afraid for their lives in a situation like this? It was just too much to even contemplate that an asshole like this was running loose out there. She looked over at Rat to see him studying her carefully. She wasn't sure what the deal was, but something was off in his gaze.

In a sudden moment of insight, she realized that instead of being the smaller and the more reasonable of the two, he suddenly looked to be the most lethal. Maybe it was the cold glare in his eyes. Maybe it was not that he wanted to punish anybody, but that he didn't care. Just a job to be done. He wasn't into the bullying and the torture. He was all about getting the job done and getting out. That could work in her favor. However, if anything went wrong, she knew without question that he would take out anybody in his way. So, in this situation, it would potentially be her. He wouldn't even think about it. She would be done and gone.

She managed to control her tears, just sitting and waiting, with her eyes open. She didn't dare take too many more blows like that last one because her brain surely had to be impacted in some way. Yet it was less about that than the damn headache that grew every time Gravelly punched her. She'd lost count of how many blows. Six maybe at this point? That she was even still conscious amazed her, though, in some ways, it would be nice to be unconscious, not enduring this and whatever else was to come. She didn't like the way Gravelly looked at her. She didn't like anything about this asshole, but the fact that Rat couldn't care less if she even existed scared her even more. She didn't care to look at them but was too scared to look away.

Her gaze flicked past the window and froze. Then she quickly switched to look at the men. She wasn't sure what she had seen but couldn't risk another look. Still she took another quick glance at the window, but the image she thought she had seen was gone. Defeated, she sank back in a dazed stupor, resigned to wait for whatever came next.

MASTERS WONDERED IF Elizabeth had seen him. He thought maybe she had, but, when she looked away again, it was almost as if she didn't see him. Even from outside, he could see her face was swollen and discolored, and he felt that immediate sense of wanting somebody to pay for having hurt her. He wasn't planning on killing these guys. Yet, when they obviously had no respect for life, he highly suspected there would be a fight to the finish before this night was over.

He'd already texted Jasper about what he'd found and was waiting for a response, as he checked out to see just how many men were involved. So far, he only saw two, but that was an easy mistake to make, and he didn't dare underestimate the situation, not with Elizabeth's life on the line. They were waiting for something or somebody, and Masters highly suspected it was him. He frantically cast around in his mind, figuring out why they would want him, and the only thing he could come up with was that stupid USB key. He wondered if still something else was on it that they hadn't found.

He sent another message back to Jasper about the key.

He finally got a text back.

On my way. Stay out of it until I get there, if you can.

He sent an affirmative back, aware that waiting wouldn't be easy. However, it could improve the outcome if things would stay as they were for the time it took Jasper to get here. It looked as if things wouldn't go to hell and back in the next few minutes, but, if that changed, Masters would have to intervene. No way he would leave her to be beaten, when she'd already been through so much.

He knew she was terrified, but she was also holding, and that was huge. She was clearly injured, but he didn't know how badly, and he didn't know if she could make a run for it. She was tied up in a chair, so Masters had to assume that she was bound at the ankles and tied up with her hands behind her. No telling how long she had been held there. With her circulation cut off to her legs, she couldn't walk, much less run.

Instead of relaxing with her eyes closed or staring at her kidnappers in an absolute and utmost panic, she was searching, as if trying not to let anybody know what she was doing. It was an interesting response from a civilian taken captive in her own home. One he appreciated because it also meant that she was thinking, that she wasn't in full panic mode. She was still sorting out what was going on and how to get out of this, and that was worth everything.

He walked around to the other window, checking to make sure he hadn't missed anything, hoping that Jasper would get here soon, when he heard one of the men speaking again.

"Screw it. I don't like this. I suggest we just go now."

Masters didn't hear what the response was, but a lot of

yelling ensued, yelling between the two men. He knew that, if things got ugly, they could either take her with them or shoot her as being too much baggage. However, if this was the same group connected to her missing brother, they'd already kept him in captivity for a long time, so that was a good thing for Elizabeth right now.

What was a bad thing was even contemplating losing her at this stage. That wouldn't happen. Suddenly gunfire blew out the window near him, and one of the men took off running for the front door. Masters bolted in the back door to see the bigger man on the ground, moaning, clutching his bleeding belly. Masters kicked the gun free of his hand and looked down at him. "Where did your buddy go?" Masters asked in a hard voice.

The other guy looked up at him and spat, "Fuck you."

Masters kicked him hard in the gut. "That's for Elizabeth." Then he quickly undid her. "What happened?" he asked.

She stared at him for a long moment. "I'm not sure. They had an argument, and this guy on the floor had always been pushing a little too much, a little too far. Then I think his partner just snapped under the pressure. Or maybe he just decided to cut his losses by shooting his partner. I don't know," she stated, staring at him in disbelief. "That was you out there, wasn't it?"

"Yep, it sure was. The thing is, we need to know if he's still around."

She winced. "Go then. Go after him."

"No, I'm not leaving you alone," he replied.

She picked up the big man's gun and announced, "I'll go lock myself in my bedroom. You go after that other asshole but make sure you identify yourself when you come back."

He hesitated, and she glared at him. "Go. He might have information about my brother."

Wincing at that, he booked it down the street, knowing that, by rights, the other guy should already be long gone. As he made it to the alleyway, he turned and kept on going. He hadn't heard a vehicle leave. He hadn't heard anything yet. Aware that he could be running straight into open gunfire, his instincts had him slowing, as he approached the corner of the neighbor's fence. He wasn't sure what was going on, but, as he crept closer, he heard a laugh.

"I figured you were there," the other gunman said in a conversational tone.

Masters replied, "Come around the corner and get yourself five in the belly."

"Only if you shoot better than I do," the gunman stated, his voice hard.

"Somehow I doubt that," Masters said.

At that, the gunman laughed and laughed. "You military guys always think you're so damn tough. You're not tough. You're just pieces of shit. Y'all think you're self-righteous do-gooders, but you don't know the half of it."

"Is that why you shot your partner?" Masters asked.

"God, he just went on and on. Besides, I knew that his beating up your girlfriend was gonna get us in trouble," he noted. "So I just took the short way out. You're welcome by the way."

Masters' eyebrows shot up. "What did you want with her?"

"I'm not gonna get anything out of her now," he admitted.

"And what about your partner?"

"Shoot him. Finish him off," he suggested. "I gut-shot

shot him, so, if you wait long enough, chances are he won't make it anyway, which is a good thing. The guy's a menace. He just wants the murder and mayhem."

"And you, what do you want?" Masters asked.

"The paycheck," he shared cheerfully. "That's all I'm in it for. Give me the paycheck, and I'm a happy camper. Screw me over on that paycheck, and I will get it back."

"And who's paying you?"

He laughed again. "I'm not stupid. Just because I'm a hired gun doesn't mean I'm missing brain cells," he said, with a sneer. "Letting out that information will be the end of me."

"You don't think this will be the end of you anyway?"

"Maybe. It could be. I don't know. I haven't worked with these guys before. But that is an interesting concept, so I'll have to keep it in mind."

"They've already killed several local hires," Masters murmured, "so you may want to hop a quick train out."

"You would like that, wouldn't you?" he asked. "One less to kill."

"One less to hunt down, yeah," Masters agreed.

"I don't know that you would let it go though because we did hurt your girlfriend," he noted. "However, she's alive, and she's not badly hurt."

"That may be true. Good thing I got here when I did."

"I saw you at the window. So, I knew where you were at. I just didn't know how many you'd brought with you. You better put a stop to all this pretty fast. They have what seems to be unlimited money," he murmured.

"Yeah, you wanna help me with a little more information than that?"

"No, I don't, not unless you got money to pay me."

"You probably want bigger money than any of us have."

"That's why I work with these kinds of people," the gunman pointed out. "They're the ones with the big bucks. So, if you ain't prepared to pay that money, I can't—"

"What was the job?" Masters interrupted him.

"Bring you in."

"Just me?" he asked.

"Yeah, you. She was collateral damage."

"So, this has nothing to do with her brother?"

"Don't know anything about her brother," he replied. "Got nothing to do with a brother, as far as I know. ... Unless it's that Nicholas guy. If that's her brother, then, yeah, it's got something to do with him, but I don't know what."

"Okay. Thanks for that much anyway."

"Oh, it's not like it's gonna help. Besides, the brother's almost dead."

"Did you see him?"

"I saw him. He's not doing so good, but then they haven't been treating him all that well."

"Do you know what they want?"

"No, I sure don't. Not my business and above my paygrade, at least until somebody gives me a promotion. I don't wanna know either."

Masters winced at that but understood the guy's philosophy, as it was common within the mercenary world. "I suppose you don't know why they've got Nicholas, *huh?*"

"Nope, sure don't."

"And you don't know why they wanted me?"

"Nope, sure don't. Explanations don't get me a paycheck."

"No, they might not get you a paycheck," Masters clarified, "but you're not the guy to go into something without knowing how to get out of it."

A silent moment of surprise came over the gunman. "Aren't you clever?"

"No, but I've met your type. You do this for money, but there's no paycheck if you don't have a way to escape the cheaters in the world."

"Cheaters in my world get themselves killed," he declared. "Maybe not today, maybe not tomorrow, but you can bet they'll pay at some point in time."

"I hear you," Masters noted, keeping the conversation going in some direction that might give him some information. "You do realize that Nicholas was looking into another guy's case. A guy who had been wrongfully convicted, had served time, and then was killed in jail."

"Sounds like a setup to me."

"Exactly. And now that Nicholas found evidence proving that people, likely higher-up brass," Masters added, "might have had something to do with it, Nicholas has been taken, kidnapped. What we don't know is what they want from him."

"They're gonna want whatever evidence he had obviously," the gunman said, with a laugh. "But what's in it for me?"

"I won't come back and kill you," Masters declared. "That might be worth something."

After a moment of silence, the guy muttered, "You're gonna hound this to the very end, aren't you?"

"Oh, I'm gonna hound it," Masters confirmed. "I don't know whether this has to do with Nicholas or somebody else we're looking at, but you can bet that we're gonna hound this right to the ground. So, if you're part of it, you're a dead man walking. You just don't know it yet."

Masters waited a beat, then sensing a change in the air, he peered ever-so-slightly around the fence corner, only to find that the gunman was gone. On the ground though, he'd left something. Masters picked it up and looked at it. His eyebrows shot straight up, and he hurried back inside to Elizabeth.

CHAPTER 12

E LIZABETH STILL SHIVERED, even huddled up against
Masters, as the two of them stood near the front
window. When a couple vehicles drove up, they'd only been
minutes behind Masters, so she realized that it had to be part
of his team, but she couldn't even begin to trust anybody at
this point.

Masters kept an arm securely around her and whispered,
"You'll be fine."

She looked up at him. "If you say so," she muttered.

Masters watched as the man approached. Then Masters
opened the front door and introduced him to Elizabeth.

This was Masters's boss, Jasper, that he met with all the
time. She smiled and nodded. "Hey."

He gave her a concerned look. "Looks like we need to
get you checked out at the hospital. That facial bruising
looks pretty-darn severe."

She gave him a flat stare and replied, "Not a big fan of
hospitals."

"Not a big fan of them myself," Jasper replied in an un-
relenting tone. "Doesn't mean we'll be stupid about not
getting you the right care though." She glared at him, and he
smiled. "Besides, a woman named Tesla would like to meet

you."

Elizabeth frowned at that. "That's the woman you were talking about, isn't it?" she asked, turning to look at Masters.

He nodded. "Yes, and she's at the hospital with her husband."

"I don't want to disturb her," she stated, "and I'm certainly not going in looking like this."

Jasper smiled. "Tesla would appreciate that even more, as she's been to hell and back herself."

Elizabeth frowned, but it was clear the two of them weren't giving her any chance to argue. Then another vehicle arrived, as did a team all in white coveralls, pushing a gurney. She cast one final glance back at Gravelly, who had died on her kitchen floor, while she'd been locked up in her room. It was hard to feel any sympathy for him. Yet she wasn't the person to wish ill on anybody.

However, she did wish that she had gotten a few licks in herself before he'd passed out. Resolutely she turned to look at Gravelly. He had paid the ultimate price, and she had to be satisfied with that. She let Masters lead her out of her house, and he carried a bag he'd packed for her. She took one last look at her house and shrugged, shaking her head.

"No matter what's going on," he reminded her, "just remember that the intel says your brother's alive."

She brightened, then looked over at him with gratitude. "The fact that you even got that much out of the gunman is pretty amazing."

"Yet we can't necessarily trust it."

"I know. I know," she said. "Don't hold my breath, but, hey, for the first time, there's some real hope."

"There's more than hope," Masters noted, "but we have to get to him, and we have to get to him fast."

"Meaning that we need to get there before they decide that this mess has gone too far."

"Exactly. They can't afford to keep him alive after this."

She winced and nodded. "Go do what you need to do," she said. "You can't just sit at the hospital and keep me company."

"I'll leave you under guard, along with Tesla, Mason's partner."

Whatever he planned to do, Elizabeth figured that he wouldn't tell her, and she also wasn't sure if she even wanted to know. She decided that it was better to let him go do whatever he needed to do. If she saw him again, well, great, perfect. And, if he didn't want anything to do with her after all this, that was also great. Hell no, it wasn't great, but she would be an adult about it. Groaning at herself and her convoluted thought processes, she sat in the front seat of the car, wishing her head didn't hurt so bad.

As if reading her thoughts, he murmured, "You let the doctors look after you, okay? They might even admit you."

"I doubt it. I'm not that bad," she muttered.

"You're not that good either," he pointed out.

She wouldn't argue with him. It took way too much energy. By the time she got to the hospital, they had to wait to be seen, and Masters was getting antsy. She waved a hand at him and said, "Go on. I don't know what it is that you've got to do, but you need to go."

He hesitated. "I do need to go." He looked around, and then relief washed over his face, as somebody else walked into the emergency room waiting area. He cried out, "Hale."

The man turned and walked in their direction. Masters stepped forward and spoke to the man, and then he returned to Elizabeth and gave her a hard kiss on the lips, completely out of the blue. "I'll be back." With that, he was gone.

Elizabeth watched Masters leave, then stared at the newcomer.

He smiled at her. "Hey, I've seen a face like that before too."

"On another person, I presume," she replied in a half-joking manner.

"Oh, I've given out a few faces like that," he noted cheerfully, "but I've also taken in my fair share of them too."

She nodded. "Did you get put on babysitting duty?"

He burst out laughing. "It's not babysitting duty, as much as safeguarding someone important."

Her eyebrows shot up at that, and she shook her head. "Okay, so that's a mixed message. I think you'd better go get that clarified."

"Don't need to," Hale stated, with a smile. "Absolutely don't need to."

She wasn't sure what he was grinning about, so she added, "I don't want you to get the wrong idea."

"Oh, I've already got the right idea," he stated. "You might not be totally on board yet, but you will be."

"And why is that?" she asked, confused.

Maybe it was her headache. Maybe it was something else. She didn't know, but the grin on his face was way too much to deal with. He just continued to smile at her and then nodded, as a nurse shuffled them to a curtained-off area. A doctor walked in shortly thereafter. Hale whispered, "We'll talk about that later."

The doctor took one look at her face, then frowned, and started ordering a bunch of tests.

She groaned as she realized she would be here for hours and hours, but Hale just patted her hand and reminded her,

"That's why we're here. We want to confirm that you are taken care of and that you don't have any lasting effects from this."

"You mean, outside of never wanting to be alone in a house again, never wanting to be the first to walk into a house, being afraid of every unlit room that I can't see into, and, well, I could go on and on."

"You could," Hale agreed. "As time goes on, you won't get any less worried, but you'll be less reactive about it."

She pondered that, as the doctor went through his physical checks, and then she was run from room to room, fulfilling all the tests that needed to be done. By the time the doctor returned to go over the results with her, he was a whole lot happier.

"No lasting brain damage," he shared, "so that's all good."

She thought of a couple comments she could have made to him but figured that nobody wanted to hear from her.

Then he went on and on about there being a fair bit of broken facial bones, *blah-blah-blah*. "But ultimately you'll be fine. What you need most right now is rest." He looked over at Hale and frowned.

Hale nodded. "Yeah, she's connected."

"*Great*. How many other people will you send me tonight?" he asked in exasperation.

"Hopefully nobody else, but I can't guarantee that."

The doctor shook his head. He studied her face again for a long time and added, "I don't like that your nasal passages, your airways, are damaged and swollen already. It won't require surgery," he shared, "but I am concerned about that swelling getting worse, and you having significant trouble breathing, so I want to keep you here overnight."

And, with that, she groaned. When he glared at her, she smiled. "Thank you very much for looking after me."

He appeared appeased at that, but shot Hale a look.

Hale grinned. "None of us like being stuck in the hospital."

"I know, but it would be good if you people would try it once in a while."

"Right," Hale replied cheerfully.

And, with that, the doctor wrote something else on his notepad and disappeared.

She looked over at Hale. "What was that all about?"

"He's used to patching up a bunch of us," Hale explained. "Not to worry, as you're in the best of hands."

"If you say so ... I wasn't sure when he mentioned broken bones."

"It seems you've got broken bones around your nose, but, since everything is in the right position, they'll splint it to make sure it heals in the correct way. And, because of that damage, he wants to keep you overnight to make sure that any increase in swelling doesn't compromise your breathing."

She winced at that thought. "Right."

"So, we will take the prudent route," Hale noted, with a smile, "and keep you here."

"I wasn't aware I had an option."

"You don't really, but we like to make you think you do." She rolled her eyes at that, and he laughed. "You might as well get used to it. None of the guys in our world are any easier to get along with."

She frowned. "I don't understand."

"I know you don't," Hale said, with a chuckle, "but you will."

"Says you."

He burst out laughing again. "We like some fire and brimstone in our women too."

When she stared at him, he just held up his hands. "It's all right," he said. "You just joined the ranks of the Keepers."

She shook her head. "You're not making any sense."

But his grin was wide and infectious. "You'll get it later."

"Sure I will," she muttered. She snuggled deeper under the covers, feeling a chill settle in.

He nodded. "The cold is all part and parcel of the injuries," he explained. "So you just rest now and know I'll be right here. We'll get you into your hospital room soon, and you'll be in here for tonight at least."

She hesitated and then asked, "Is being in here safe?"

"It is safe," he confirmed, "and we've doubled up the guards."

Her eyebrows shot high at that.

He nodded. "Mason's here. With already one attempt on his life, we will not tolerate a second," he declared. And, with that, he smiled. "I'll be back in a few minutes." Then he turned and walked out of the room.

The whole time he was gone, all she could do was wonder what the hell he meant by *the Keepers*.

MASTERS WALKED INTO the department to find several of the men already gathered here, including Jasper and the often missing Lichen.

Jasper looked up and gave him a quick nod. "The address is a warehouse toward the docks," he shared.

"Figures. That would be a standard location for these guys."

"I still don't understand how you figured this out," Sam snapped, glaring at Masters. "And why the hell you can't tell us what the goddamn address is."

Masters just stared at him, until the other man looked away. The last thing Masters wanted to do was get into a fight over who was in the right and who was in the wrong on something like this—at least not right now. Masters was still surprised that the one gunman had dropped this clue on his way out of town.

Jasper replied, "Nobody in this room, except for me and Masters, knows the address. You are all under suspicion, until proven we can trust you."

That had Sam cursing, but Morgan told him to shut his trap. Lichen never seemed to speak, so he looked on silently, sending frowns to Sam, then to Morgan.

Masters looked over at Jasper. "She's got a broken nose and a few other injuries," he shared, his tone tight. "Hale is on guard duty."

Jasper nodded. "Good, at least we know that's covered, and we can focus on the rest."

Masters nodded at that. "Still doesn't change the fact that I want to be in on this." When Jasper hesitated, Masters added, "If it was you, you would feel the same way."

"I just can't have you going off half-cocked."

"The last time I went off half-cocked was, … let me think about it," he began in a steely voice. "Oh, wait, … never."

Jasper chuckled. "Okay, fine. You convinced me. I'll deal with the brass afterward."

"Are they the ones who kept me out?" Masters asked.

Jasper nodded. "Definitely a topic of discussion."

"All the more reason to let me in," Masters declared.

"On that point, I agree with you," he muttered. He looked around at the others. "Anybody here inclined to cause me trouble over that?"

The three other men looked at each other, then back at Jasper and shrugged.

"You seem to be calling the shots, so, if you get your ass kicked over this, what do I care?" Sam sneered at Masters.

That was probably the best they would get out of him.

Jasper gave him a hard look. "You have a reckoning coming," he warned, "but I don't have time to kick your ass right now. We gathered as much intel on Nicholas as we could today, but we're under the gun here. So we're pulling in as much as we can about the building and the owners. Plus I've got a SWAT team being pulled together," he told the others.

"Not fast enough," Masters muttered in frustration.

"For you, nothing will be fast enough," Jasper conceded, "but we also know the bottom line of what's going on here."

"I still don't understand how the hell we went from working on Mason's case to working on Nicholas's case," Sam snapped.

"Do you have a problem with finding your missing team member?" Morgan asked, as he looked at his coworker.

"No, I don't. I just don't understand, one, how we missed this. We thought he was dead and didn't have any intel to show otherwise. And, two, I don't understand how we went so completely off the rail in our Nicholas investigation that it could connect with Mason's case."

"We didn't go off the rail," Jasper corrected. "We took a side path. Mason's case is still very much a priority, but we can't ignore the fact that Nicholas has been held captive for four fucking months because nobody saw fit to direct his case properly."

At that, Sam glared at him and snapped, "It's not our fault. We were told to lay off."

"Oh, I hear you," Jasper snapped right back. "And that will be something I deal with very quickly after this rescue. But, in the meantime, I need to know if you're playing some game, if you'll just cry wolf to somebody higher up."

"I probably should," Sam replied, glaring at him. "You're going against a direct rule."

"Yep, I absolutely am, so go ahead and call whoever called you off Nicholas's investigation," Jasper suggested, tossing his phone to Sam. "Then we'll have a serious look as to why you walked away from your missing coworker's case and why you haven't been here on overtime every fucking day and night since then, finding this poor guy. Instead you went home to your nice, cushy little world every day. Meanwhile Nicholas has been suffering, hoping that his team had his back."

At that, Sam flushed, set Jasper's phone on his desk, then retired back to his seat.

Morgan nodded. "We already feel bad enough."

"Not nearly as bad as Nicholas must be feeling. So not nearly bad enough, if you ask me," Jasper snapped. "We'll discuss that afterward too, but, right now, I need to know if your team is on board to saving your own goddamn team member or if you'll spit in this kettle and ruin the entire soup."

"No, we're there," Morgan replied. "We are."

"Other than my hand-picked team, I don't believe anybody anymore," Jasper spat, his gaze turning from one to the other. As everybody settled in, Jasper went over the plans. "We have a full Tactical Unit coming in to breach the warehouse property," he explained, "but we need more intel, so I want two of you to go in."

Immediately Masters stood up. "Me." He turned to face the three traitors in their midst. "Alone."

Jasper frowned at him.

"Don't. Don't even argue," Masters muttered. "You already know I'm the best guy for the job, so I'm going in first. Where do you want me to enter, and what is it I'm looking for?"

"The usual," Jasper replied. "I need to know how many men we are dealing with. I don't want anybody else killed on this job." He turned to address the others. "The bad news is that we'll need an ambulance standing by for Nicholas. The information Masters brought in is that Nicholas is in rough shape."

"According to the gunman, so not confirmed," Masters added.

"At what point in time," Sam interrupted, "are you gonna tell us about this cozy little talk you had with this gunman?"

"Maybe after we get Nicholas back and to the hospital, finally getting medical treatment," Masters declared, turning to glare at Sam. "Until then, you don't deserve more consideration." And, with that, he turned back to Jasper and asked, "What's the plan for timing?"

"We're moving out in forty-five."

Masters frowned and shook his head. "Let me go in now. I can relay back any intel to you."

Jasper hesitated.

"It's the best way. I could be in and out in less than thirty. We could have an empty warehouse, and we could have Nicholas rescued and in the hospital within forty-five minutes."

Jasper shrugged, rubbing his forehead. "That this needs to be—"

"Surgical. I know," he said, interrupting his friend. "I know exactly what this needs to be." Masters turned and looked at the other guys, just wanting to say something, then shook his head. He looked back at Jasper. "Make sure you're keeping an eye on these three too."

Jasper nodded.

Then Masters turned and walked out. He quickly headed home, where he kept a full set of blackout gear. He didn't have much in the way of weapons, but he could certainly access what he needed. He had his personal weapon, and that was the one he was most comfortable with. He loaded up a few extra shells, grabbed his gloves, helmet, and added the bulletproof vest. He wouldn't be a hero in this situation, not when so much of a question remained in terms of who was on which side. He drove carefully to the dock area and parked a full mile and a half away in a mall parking lot, full of late-night shoppers.

Donning a yellow windbreaker, he covered up anything that didn't make him look like a completely innocent shopper. When he headed to the back alley, he ditched the bright yellow jacket and moved quickly toward the warehouse. When he approached from the side and could see it up ahead, he sent a quick message to Jasper to confirm Masters had arrived. He assessed the warehouse from the outside carefully, listening for any voices, any sounds, traffic, anything at all. But there was nothing. It was dead. He winced at the term because the last thing he wanted was to find Elizabeth's brother dead. That would be the end none of them wanted.

As he sat here, studying the situation, a vehicle exited the warehouse and drove casually away. He snagged what he could from the license plate and sent them to Jasper. The metal bay doors closed behind the vehicle, and, with any luck, just one guard was on duty, and only one. He moved smoothly to the warehouse, but everything appeared to be locked up tight.

He checked for security cameras. One was at the front entrance, nothing on the side, and one at the back, where the loading area was. However, he found a window ever-so-slightly ajar. With that window open, the security system couldn't be properly activated—or else no sensor was on the window itself.

After a quick check with his fingers, he couldn't find a sensor. So, taking a chance, he slowly pushed open the window. When no alarms went off, he smiled and jumped in through the window. Inside, he sent an updated text to Jasper and slowly moved through the warehouse, floor by floor. By the time he'd gone all the way up and back down, he only had the basement left to search. He shook his head. Everybody did evil shit like this in the basement.

He'd already sent an all clear except for the basement back to Jasper. By now, Jasper and a full team were collecting somewhere nearby. As Masters slid quietly down the stairs, he noted an unnatural stillness. He froze, knowing that this floor was not unoccupied. It was most definitely occupied, but Masters didn't know how many to expect and whether they knew that he was already here. He slid into the shadows and stayed for a long minute, as he waited and assessed the place.

Up ahead, he heard mechanical voices, but he wasn't close enough to hear the words. He listened some more and then crept forward ever-so-slightly. He got about four feet ahead, when he realized the noises came from a TV. It could just be there for the guards. Or was this just extra noise to help ease a long night ahead? He wasn't sure, but it made him even more wary.

As he crept even closer to the TV room, he heard the words better and recognized the sound of some game show. He didn't understand why anybody watched those, but he knew they were popular all around. As he studied the area, he thought he heard a *bang* up ahead. He slipped back into the shadows and waited. When nothing else came, he moved forward again. And again came another *bang*.

He stayed where he was, waiting, but it seemed to be a door slamming, although it might have been a door opening, then slamming shut just from the wind. It was hard to say, but every sound seemed to echo. Shifting a little more, he crept a little closer. No way to see into the TV room, unless he looked through the window in the door, and that was taking a chance. Still, he needed to know.

If that was where the guards were, Masters could take them out right now. He slipped ever closer, peered in through the small window in the door, and saw the TV, a small kitchenette, and living space but no guard. Yet one jacket was on the back of a chair, and a solo coffee cup remained on the table. He slipped down into the darkness of the hallway and waited. At least one guard was on duty, but there should have been more. However, if only one, Masters would take his chances and be grateful. The fact was, no way they would have left a prisoner with only one guard on him, unless they thought that it was completely safe, completely secure, and that nobody could tell anything about what was going on here.

Masters couldn't take that chance and had to make sure. He needed to share the most intel possible with Jasper, in the time allotted to him.

As he continued down the hallway, he came to one of four closed doors, with absolutely no markings on the outside, no way to know what was on the inside. Just four solid doors. If he opened one of these doors, somebody could be behind it, his gun in hand and his finger on the trigger. If Masters opened a door that triggered an alarm, it would be all over. If he opened a door, and the guard was there, that would also completely halt everything Masters was doing.

Masters hesitated, waiting a moment, then, hearing a toilet flush, he stood on the hinged side of the door. It opened, and a guard came out, turning right for him. The guard stopped, surprise on his face. Masters swung, hard and sure, and the guard didn't even see it coming. He dropped the man where he stood. The guy was huge. By the time Masters dragged his prisoner back into the washroom and shut the door behind him, he was sweating.

"Damn it, man," he muttered to himself. "Definitely time to lay off the McDonald's."

He silently raced to the next door, listened at it, and, hearing nothing, quickly opened it and found the room empty. He went to the next one, which was empty as well, then the next one, which was locked. He stared at it and tapped on it ever-so-lightly. He heard the slightest of movements. He pulled his lockpick set from his back pocket and very quickly had the door open and stepped inside. There on a bed lay a man, his face almost unrecognizable from the beatings he'd sustained.

Masters raced to his bedside and whispered, "Nicholas? Your sister wants you to bring ice cream."

The guy's eyes lit up, and he nodded ever-so-slightly.

"Okay, good. I'm here alone, but the team's coming. How many guards are here?"

Nicholas whispered, "Usually four."

"I saw a vehicle leave," he muttered, "and I've taken out one."

Nicholas appeared to consider that but obviously was struggling, either with information or he just didn't know.

"Hang on," Masters whispered, hearing another set of footsteps. He quickly stepped out of the room and went across to the washroom. The first guard was still here, still unconscious. Masters stepped inside and closed and locked the door and waited. A moment later, somebody banged on the door.

"Get the hell out of there, Gunter. I told you before, stop taking so goddamn long. Other people have to take a shit too." Then grumbling, he headed down the hallway.

Smiling, Masters opened the door ever-so-slightly, then stepped into the hallway, seeing the other man disappear ahead of him into the TV room. He had a split second to decide whether he'd take on the second guard in the TV room or just take Nicholas and make a run for it. Deciding to take out the second guard, Masters raced to the TV room.

As he stepped inside, a metal barrel landed against his forehead, and a gravelly voice muttered, "Don't move, asshole."

Masters froze, then shifted so he could see the face of the man beside him.

The second guard grinned. "Yeah, it's always a good idea to face your maker, but no pleading for your life, please. I don't give a shit."

"Got it," Masters replied, with a nod. "Seems like you

and your buddies are all the same."

"Damn right. It's the paycheck. You have to earn one somehow."

While he was still talking, Masters drew from his martial arts skills and dropped him where he stood.

He stared down at the second guard, even as he picked up the guard's gun. "You might have to earn a paycheck somehow, but you should do an equally good job to keep it. Somehow I think you are gonna get terminated." Masters gathered the first guard from the bathroom and put him with his buddy in the TV room. After tying both up to separate chairs, he covered the window on the door with newsprint, then locked the TV room door from the outside with one of the keys found on the guards.

Masters hurried back to Nicholas, confirming he was still alive. "Can you walk?"

Nicholas, his voice raspy and harsh, said, "Not sure. Don't think so."

"Right, I got you," Masters replied. "I've already sent a message to the team. I'll take you out of here, and if we're lucky—"

"No, I'm, … I'm not sure that—"

"If we're lucky, we'll get the hell out of here. If not, I'll stash you somewhere, but I'll come back. You got that?"

Nicholas nodded. "Thanks, man."

"Don't thank me. Better thank your sister."

"Is Elizabeth okay?" he asked.

"Yeah. She even tried to sue the military to get answers."

A smile, the first that he'd seen out of Nicholas, revealed a hint of the strong and handsome man who Nicholas was, despite months of starvation and torture. He had a great smile, even with some of his teeth missing. "She's good people," he whispered, clearly in pain.

"I know, and I should tell you that I've got designs on her myself."

"What?"

Masters chuckled. "Don't worry. We'll deal with that later. In the meantime, no easy way to get you out of here. I've got to just pack you and run, and it'll hurt like hell."

The other man paled and nodded, but Masters quickly scooped him up in a fireman's lift over his shoulder, and, taking one last look around, raced back the way he'd come.

CHAPTER 13

E LIZABETH OPENED HER eyes, wincing at the pain from just that single small movement. Even still, it took her a moment to comprehend what she saw in front of her, but, sure enough, Masters was pushing someone in a wheelchair. As soon as she saw Nicholas, she bolted from bed and raced for him.

Masters held up a hand, stopping her from throwing herself at her brother. "Easy. I only brought him up here so you could see for yourself and would know that he's alive, but I've got to get him down to the ER now."

She shoved a fist in her mouth to stop the cries, as she turned to stare at her brother, whose face looked far worse than her own, and she hadn't even thought that was possible. "Oh my God, Nicholas," she whispered.

His lips twitched, as he smiled. "I'll survive."

Tears in her eyes, she watched as Masters turned the wheelchair around and headed out the door. "Get your ass back in bed now," he ordered her, "and I'll return as soon as I can with updates. In the meantime, know that he's alive and that he's getting help." And, with that, he and her brother were gone.

She slowly crawled back into bed, suddenly exhausted.

They'd admitted her last night, even though she shouldn't have been surprised. Apparently something about head injuries needing to be monitored, *blah-blah-blah*. She wasn't even sure what that was all about, but now that she was here, she didn't even know what to say. She was completely overwhelmed to think that her brother was safe and alive and here at the base hospital with her.

She waited on tenterhooks, until she realized it would likely be a while before Masters returned. In between, she had nurses and doctors in and out of her hospital room, and the doctors agreed that she could leave later today, but they needed to run a few more tests first. If everything was clear, then she would get released. She knew that the minute she left to go do tests, Masters would show up, but still she saw no sign of him hours later, when she had finally been wheeled back into her room. She sent him a text, asking if everything was okay.

Be there in a few minutes.

She winced at that because it wasn't a yes, and it wasn't a no. It was more like a *We don't know yet*. And considering what she'd seen of her brother, she couldn't even imagine. But he'd recognized her, and he'd whispered, *Hey, sis*, so he knew who she was. Now all she could think about was getting down there to him. She knew she wouldn't be allowed to touch him, and something crazy like giving him a hug would be out of the question. But just knowing he was alive made everything okay. She had finally relaxed back in the bed, just when the door opened, and Masters came inside, holding two cups of coffee. She stared at him, and the tears started flowing.

"Hey, hey, hey," he murmured. He put down the cups and gave her a big hug. He held her close and whispered,

"It's all right. It's okay. We'll get through this."

She nodded, but the tears wouldn't stop.

He sat down on the bed and pulled her into his arms, so she was half sitting in his lap, and he rocked her. Just that simple comfort, knowing that somebody gave a damn, had listened to her, and had gone the extra mile to help her brother, it was, … it was everything.

When the tears finally dried up, she whispered, "I'm so sorry. I'm sure that's not what you needed."

He chuckled and pushed the hair off her damp face and asked, "Why? You're sorry for being human?"

Her lips quirked at that. "Is that what that was? Being human?"

"You just saw your brother, who has been missing and you had thought quite possibly dead for months," he replied. "He's alive and he'll recover, though he may need some extra surgeries," he shared. "He's had several broken bones that have been left to heal without being set properly, so he'll need some corrective surgery."

She listened to every word and nodded. "They tortured him, didn't they?"

"Yes, though I think it was more of a pastime than anything more specific than that," he explained. "I got delayed, caught up in the military investigations, as everybody is scrambling to figure out what happened to Nicholas and why, and are all talking to him."

"But Nicholas is not talking, is he?"

"He can't talk right now. He's gone in for surgery. He's got a few injuries that needed fixing right away."

She winced and nodded. "And you mentioned more surgeries afterward."

"Most likely, yes," he confirmed. "They've gone in to fix

a displaced and cracked rib that's scraping against his lung, and another rib that's completely broken and may need to have pieces removed. His leg needs to be reset, but I don't know whether they'll try do that in this same surgery or not," he noted. "We'll have to wait and hear what the doctor says."

"Anything *major*-major?"

"He has some internal bleeding, and they're not sure what's causing that, but it's not so bad that it's the highest priority. There was some thought that his spleen is potentially damaged and needs to come out, but again let them go in and look, then figure out what all happened. He's getting the best care possible right now. You did everything you could, and you didn't give up, and this time it was enough."

She looked up at him and shook her head. "This time *you* were enough."

He smiled. "No need to go over who did what. The fact of the matter is, we found your brother and got him out of there."

"And that was away from Rat?" When he frowned, she flushed. "The two guys who held me captive at my place, I named one of them Rat, and the other one was Gravelly."

"And of course Gravelly's the dead one."

"Right."

"We were able to find out some things. The dead guy," he began, "his name is Jim, and he's an ex-Marine. He was discharged about four years ago."

"A Marine?" she repeated, staring at Masters and shaking her head.

"An ex-Marine, dishonorably discharged," he clarified.

"And what did he do?"

"He attacked several women on base, with zero remorse, and thought he should be allowed to do what he wanted because he was a Marine."

"Yeah, he had that attitude," she murmured. "He was a complete asshole. That does make sense, and I'd gotten the impression that an awful lot of women had suffered at his hands."

"We'll do a full dive into his background to see just what shit he's been up to, and, hopefully, if other people need help or have had problems with Jim, maybe we can bring some closure for them too."

She nodded slowly, not at all sure about that. Finding people was one thing, but getting them to talk was another, although finding out that this women-beating guy was dead and not able to come back and hurt anybody again would be huge news. She settled back. "You found Nicholas," she muttered in wonder.

"I did, but honestly it was all because of Rat sharing that detail with me, not because we had any intel that gave us any insight into where Nicholas was being held."

She smiled, and then her smile fell away. "Will you get in trouble for letting Rat go?"

"Not considering we got this boon and brought back one of our men. I shouldn't think so anyway." And then he shrugged. "Doesn't matter. It was a decision I made in the moment."

"I suppose you could have killed him, couldn't you?"

"Possibly. Or I could have also taken a bullet myself."

She winced at that and shook her head. "I think there's been enough violence."

"Maybe. I'm not too bothered by Jim's death either way," he stated, his tone cool. "Not when he attacks women alone in their homes as a means to get to me."

"And all because of … what?"

"I believe they were after the USB key."

"Which means that key and all that information on it is incredibly important."

"It is important," he agreed. "I'm just not sure how much of it pertains to the case that we were supposed to be working on."

She winced at that. "Of course. We're talking about Mason's shooting, right?"

He nodded. "And this has now opened up an entirely different avenue of exploration," he murmured. "Yet we still don't have any real connection to it being linked to Mason's case."

"God, his wife must be beside herself."

"She's as actively involved as she can be in keeping herself and her family safe."

"Does she have children?"

"They have one toddler, a boy, and she's about eight months pregnant," he replied, with a glance around, as if the room would tell him. Then he smiled, shook his head, and added, "I don't know—maybe she's only six months along, but she's big."

At that, Elizabeth snorted. "*Big* is not something she'll want to hear."

"No, I wouldn't dare say that to her right now," he stated, his own grin peeking out. "She's very good people though, and, anytime we need help, she's always been there."

"And yet you don't know her all that well? She's Jasper's cousin."

"No, I just met her, but I do know Mason, and I understand that, whenever we've needed someone to go the extra mile on a case, if you had a connection to Mason, it gave you a hell of a connection to Tesla."

"So that's why everybody's so friendly."

He chuckled. "No, not necessarily, but we aren't ones to have access to a gift like that and not put it to good use."

"Of course not," she murmured. "One day I'll get to meet her."

"You might get to meet her sooner than you think, as you are staying in the same hospital."

"No, no, no," she argued, tapping him on the cheek. "They were running a bunch of tests today, then told me that I could go home later today."

"Really?" he asked.

"Yes, and I'm sure I'll get that whole speech about staying home, staying in bed, *blah-blah-blah*. But more than that, I want to be here for my brother."

"And you *can* be here for your brother, at least to a certain point. I suspect that, with everything going on with him right now, the doctors may keep him sedated for a while for his body to heal and for him to have a break from the pain he's endured."

She winced. "Which means he'll essentially be in the same state as Mason."

"Yes, except I think they may start bringing Mason out in the next day or two. In your brother's case, I don't know how bad it is, though I heard mention of months of recovery."

"Probably more than that," she murmured. "I don't see how there couldn't be after four months of torture and abuse."

"That's quite possible. We just need to give him a chance. He survived. Now it's up to us to do the rest."

She smiled. "You are a nice person. More than that, you went to bat for me and my brother, when I thought everybody else had given up."

"We also had a little more intel coming through at the time."

"I still think it's a cover-up."

"I don't know if it was a cover-up as much as they had what they thought was a special case happening, and they were just keeping it under wraps. It's never a good situation when investigators go missing."

"Exactly, and yet, if you think about it, it makes perfect sense if Nicholas was onto something within his own team."

"That's what we'll look at." He smiled at her and said, "And, if you're being released, no way you're staying home alone."

"I could go to my brother's house and stay there."

"You could, but you would still be alone there too. However, that's something we'll need to get ready for him too, maybe even to accommodate a wheelchair for several months. And I still need to go there and check to see if there were any bugs." He pondered that, then nodded. "I need to do that at your place too."

She stared up at him, and it hit her. "This isn't over, is it?"

He slowly shook his head. "No, it's not over. I would love to tell you that it is, but it just isn't."

She swallowed hard as she thought about it and realized so many things could still get messed up in her world. "That sucks, yet we have some good things going on right now."

"And the good thing is, your brother is back with you, so you hang on to that," he declared. "Let the rest of us deal with the other problems."

"I'll let you deal with them, but that's only because I believe in you," she admitted. "I don't think the rest of the team is any good."

"I understand why you would say that, but don't tar Jasper with that same brush. He's a good man."

She smiled. "Okay, Jasper is allowed too."

At that came a laugh. "I'm sure glad to hear that," a man interjected from the doorway, "because I've never been considered one of the bad guys before. It would be a completely new experience."

She watched as Jasper walked in and looked over at Masters. "Good job, by the way."

Masters nodded. "It hurt to see him like that. He didn't give in, but he was so done."

"Especially after such a long time," Jasper muttered. He looked over at Elizabeth. "And good for you for still fighting the good fight for your brother."

Tears came into her eyes. "It just makes me so angry," she muttered.

He nodded. "Of course, and that anger is something you needed to get you through this, but listen, Nicholas is here, and he's safe, and now he can begin to heal. Meanwhile we will figure out what the hell happened to him and go on from here. The warehouse where he was being held is being torn apart right now." He looked back at Masters. "Nobody else was there today. And the place had already been cleaned out, including the TV," he added, with a note of humor.

Masters shrugged. "If I'd seen anybody else, I would have taken them down," he stated.

"The two men that you secured were also gone."

Masters frowned at him. "Shit, that means someone else was close enough to see me."

"I suspect so, and, if we hadn't gotten there as quickly as we did, you would have been taken out too. Still, in the process, they also managed to get their men out."

"Damn," Masters muttered. "I would have thought that the bad guys would have just killed the other bad guys and left them behind."

"Maybe they did, but they probably just didn't want us to have anything else to go by."

Masters pondered that and nodded. "It's quite possible. I don't know. I wasn't … Not a lot of time passed between my getting out with Nicholas versus you guys arriving, which means that the bad guys were there already. So they decided they wouldn't stop me, wouldn't stop you, or wouldn't take the chance of themselves being taken, and they grabbed what they could and ran?"

"It's still kind of surprising that they didn't just shoot those two guards."

"It depends if the guards were aware of what was really going on."

Jasper shrugged. "The bottom line is, we don't have any bodies to deal with, which I'll take as a good thing, and we didn't have any firefight going on in the warehouse. And now forensics is all over it."

"Of course. That's a damn good thing too."

Jasper nodded at that. "It should be fairly simple from here on in, but nothing's ever quite so simple."

"No," he muttered, "it's not." Masters looked back at Elizabeth. "She wants to get out of here."

"Sure, she does," Jasper agreed, with a smile. "She's also been to hell and back."

"Not like my brother has though," she muttered. "I'll stay here with him, if I can."

Immediately Jasper shook his head. "He'll be under full guard," he shared. "The navy's investigation department is doing everything they can to make up for having ignored Nicholas's plight all this time. Still, you have to remember that it wasn't willful ignorance on their part. They just didn't have anything to go on."

She frowned at that, then slowly shrugged. "I can forgive a lot because we found him," she clarified, "but, for that, I'm crediting Masters."

Masters shrugged. "I don't work alone. It's always a team effort."

"Maybe, but it feels like it was *your* team, not the team already on base," she declared. "I don't think they gave a crap."

"There'll be an investigation into that too," Jasper noted. "Not to worry."

She nodded. "If I can't be with Nicholas, I would love to go home and stay home, but Masters doesn't seem to think that's safe."

"Nope, it isn't. So, considering that you and Masters both need some recovery time, I suggest the two of you go home and stay there, whether at your place or Nicholas's. If you need backup or another man to stand guard so you can rest, you let me know."

Masters frowned at that.

She could see that he didn't like the idea that he might not be up to snuff, and she glared at him. "If I have to rest, you have to rest too."

He snorted. "Totally different story. You got the shit kicked out of you."

"Maybe so," she conceded, "but you've also been running on empty and need to sleep."

"Sleep I could use," he admitted, and he looked over at Jasper. "Let me take a look at her place, see if it's been trashed."

At that, she gasped and stared at him.

"We won't know anything until we get there."

"Christ, I didn't even think about that," she muttered. She looked around the room and frowned. "I would like to go, regardless of what we find. I would rather know how bad it is as soon as possible."

"Of course," Masters agreed, "but have you been released?" Then she glared at him, and he smiled. "I'll take that as a no. Let me go track down the doctor, see if we can get you out of here, and then I'll get you home again."

IT TOOK AN extra forty minutes to make that happen, but Elizabeth didn't consider that all too long in the overall scheme of things, not now that Masters drove her back to her house.

As they pulled up in the front, he studied the area carefully but couldn't see anything different.

"Satisfied?" she asked him.

"No, I'm sure not satisfied," he countered, "but I will consider where we're going and what we're up to carefully as we move forward." As he got out, he turned and added, "I know you don't want to hear this, but I want you to stay in the car with the doors locked and let me make sure the house is clear first." He grabbed the black box out of the vehicle.

Frowning, she watched as he entered her house alone. When he came out ten minutes later and waved for her to come in, she raced up to him. "No bugs in your house. We'll have to check Nicholas's house tomorrow."

She nodded. "I'm glad to hear everything's good. You

guys were pretty terrifying, talking about needing a guard."

"I'm not sure we don't," he added, "because I don't know if anybody's coming back."

"But why would they?" she cried out in astonishment. "They still didn't get the contents of the USB key, and now we have my brother." She winced. "Yet you don't think they'll just leave it at that, do you?"

"If it was me, and I was on a mission to get something, no, I sure wouldn't stop," he shared. "I also wouldn't have waited this long, and it's the waiting that I don't understand. We'll have to figure that out in order to get to the bottom of this."

He was right. It didn't make a whole lot of sense, but then none of this made sense to her. It just seemed like it was a convoluted and unnecessarily complex issue. "Maybe it had something to do with a payment," she suggested.

He frowned. "What do you mean?"

"Maybe they took Nicholas for a promise of money, and payment was never received, so they were waiting to get money from someone else. In the meantime, Nicholas just became a punching bag."

"That's possible," he noted, looking at her in approval. "The thing is, at this point we don't know. Until your brother has a chance to wake up, we don't have a way to find out, and that may not even be something he remembers."

"Four months is a long time."

"Not only a long time," he said, "but it was also a tough passage that he went through. So it is very possible that he won't remember very much at all. Beatings like that on a consistent basis just kick everything out of your brain on a permanent level. It's the only way to deal with the stress and the trauma of what you've been through." He stopped and asked her, "How are you feeling?"

She winced. "Sore, tired, puffy." She reached up and patted her face. "I'm not looking forward to seeing my face in the mirror."

"I'm surprised you haven't done so already," he teased, his face cracking into a big smile.

"It's bad, isn't it?"

"I won't say it's good because that'll get me into trouble, but I for damn sure won't say it's bad either because that'll get me into trouble as well." When she glared at him, he shrugged. "What I can tell you is that, no matter how bad it looks right now, the swelling will go down in a couple days, and it'll be back to normal."

"A couple days?" she asked, narrowing her gaze at him.

He pondered that for a few minutes and shrugged. "Okay, so maybe a little longer than that, depending on how your face heals. I don't think you're used to getting punched like that."

"No, I definitely am not," she muttered, "but thank you for being honest."

He shrugged. "No point in not being honest. Your face will heal. That's the good news, and you have your brother back, the other good news. So, everything else is minor."

She smiled. "You're right. That does put it all into per-spective."

"Good. So, as far as the other crap going on, we need to get to the bottom of your brother's case and Mason's shooting as well. It's not just me on Mason's case though, so that helps."

"Maybe, but I suspect that it'll just be you."

"No, it isn't," he clarified, with a smile. "I know a lot of good investigators, and we might need to pull in a couple.

Of course, just because I'm here doesn't mean that I won't be on call for anything else," he shared. "In the meantime, I could use some rest. I just need to know that you'll stay in the house, that you'll keep the doors locked, and that you won't leave or open the doors for any reason," he explained. "I will not sleep or rest if you can't commit to that. If you can't do that, I'll bring in somebody to watch over us." She frowned at him. He shook his head as he stroked a finger across her swollen cheek. "Some things are just too important, and right now we can't take any chances of somebody coming back around."

"And how do you think they would know?"

"Because chances are very good that they saw me on the street cameras. So, they'll recognize me as being the guy here at your house and at Nicholas's." She swore at that. He nodded. "That's one of the reasons why I must ensure that you stay safe and that everything from here on out is covered. We can't have anybody getting into these hostage situations again," he explained. "We're into rescuing, not getting beat up. I'm very aware that, if I had gotten to your house a few minutes earlier, I could have saved you a beating, at least part of it. I'm still kicking myself for meeting with Jasper as long as I did, instead of coming here and sparing you that."

He hated to see her face like it was. One eye was fully functional, but the other one was on the puffy side. Her face in general was swollen and bruised, under the splint that stabilized her nose and other facial bones. Yet she exuded this sense of euphoria because her brother was alive. He smiled. "At least you have your brother," he murmured. "So, above all else, that is what you need to hold on to."

She wrapped her arms around his waist and laid her head

against his chest.

He held her close and asked, "Now, will you promise?"

She chuckled. "What? Are you afraid that I was just doing that to avoid promising?"

"No, I wasn't afraid of anything, but now that you mentioned it …"

She smiled, still warm in the comfort of his arms, and nodded. "I promise because I agree. You need to get some quality sleep."

He smiled. "You do too. So let's lock up, head upstairs, and grab a few hours, if we can, because we have no idea how much chaos could happen after this." Then he locked the doors securely and helped her upstairs.

With a final look out the window, he urged her into her bed. "Now get some sleep. I'll be in the spare room." And with that, he slowly crept to the other room.

"The bed in the spare room isn't very comfortable," she called out.

"It'll be fine," he muttered.

He was so tired that he wasn't sure it would matter. On the other hand, he also needed to stay awake if anything happened with her. It would be better, much better, if he could stay in her bedroom with her, but he didn't want to push it.

"You could stay in here," she offered. "That way you can keep an eye on me."

He turned and asked, narrowing his gaze, "Do I need to keep an eye on you?"

"In that case, you won't sleep, will you?"

"No, I sure won't, and now you're worrying me that I'll have to call for backup."

"No, no, no," she argued. "It'll be fine. Come on and lie

down in here." When he hesitated, she smiled. "I won't take advantage of you while you sleep, I promise."

That startled a grin onto his face. "Comments like that just—"

"I promise."

"I know that's what you're saying, but—"

"And I'm not a tease, by the way," she added.

He rolled his eyes, as he sat down beside her. "Honestly, at the moment, it wouldn't matter if you were or not, because I do need some sleep."

When he tentatively stretched out on the bed beside her, she grabbed the folded blanket at the end of the bed and tossed it over him, then crawled under the top blanket on her side. "Now sleep. I promise that I won't go anywhere."

He hesitated for a brief moment, then closed his eyes and fell asleep.

CHAPTER 14

ELIZABETH WOKE FEELING surprisingly good, with
Masters still curled up beside her. She smiled, knowing
that it was an intimate experience to watch him sleep and yet
helpless to do anything else. When her phone buzzed, she
reached over to answer it, but Masters's arm swung around
her waist and pulled her back down again. She murmured,
"And here I thought you weren't awake."

"I'm not," he muttered.

She chuckled and then realized it was probably more of
an instinctive reaction. She wasn't allowed to leave or it
worried him. Considering everything he'd done for her, it
was the least she could do to stay here and allow him some
true rest. She remained still, as she watched and waited. Sure
enough he drifted deeper back under again. She curled up
beside him, her phone in her hand, and checked up on
messages and emails.

After a few minutes, he yawned beside her.

She muttered, "You should go back to sleep."

"No, I'm done now," he replied. "I just need a minute to
wake up."

"You have lots of minutes," she noted.

"Have you heard from the hospital?"

"No, but I'll call them right now." She dialed the hospital. After being on hold for a bit, she got an update on her brother's condition. When she got off the phone, her voice was subdued. "He's out of surgery, and he did fine, but he's, … he's in rough shape. I can go see him, but he won't be conscious for a while."

"No, I don't imagine he'll be conscious for *quite* a while," he replied. "Remember that part about a medically induced coma?"

"Yeah, she mentioned something about that, but he'll make it," she declared. "And that's what counts."

He wrapped an arm around her, pulled her up tightly against him, and added, "That's what you need to hang on to. Even if his rehab takes a very long time, you just hang on to the fact that he's here and that he's alive. Everything else we can fix over time."

She hugged him close and whispered, "I do appreciate that you went to bat for him."

He smiled and just held her even closer.

After a few minutes, she groaned and added, "I don't know about you, but I need food."

He chuckled. "Coffee would be good too."

"Okay. Coffee and food it is," she declared. "Are you ready to wake up?"

"I'm awake," he said. "I'm just enjoying a few minutes of downtime."

She snuggled back into his arms. "Yeah, me too."

"By the way, your brother might have a question whenever you get to talk to him."

"A question about what?"

"When I rescued him, I mentioned something to him. He seemed quite surprised, but honestly I'm not surprised at all."

Confused, she looked up at him. "You're not making a whole lot of sense."

"Oh, but I am," he stated, with a smile. "It's just that you don't know."

"I don't know what?"

"When I found Nicholas, I told him that he could thank his sister for his rescue."

"Hardly, that was all you."

"Sure, but you're the one who kept that hope active, that kept bringing it back to the forefront of everybody's mind, whether they liked it or not."

"By being a pain in the ass."

"And sometimes that is what we have to do," he noted, smiling at her. "Anyway, I also told him that we would talk later, but I had designs on his sister."

She stared at him, and the words didn't compute. "You said what?" she asked, half laughing.

"That I had designs on his sister. I got a similar reaction from him."

"Yeah, ya think?" she quipped, staring at him in disbelief. "FYI, I don't think people talk like that anymore. I haven't heard that expression in a very long time."

"Yeah, I'm a bit of a dinosaur," he admitted. "I'm a throwback to a time when words meant something and when honor and ethics and all those good things could be counted on from everyone."

"I'm glad to hear that," she replied, "because, when you put it that way, I guess maybe I'm a bit of a throwback too. You told him that?" she asked, still stunned.

He smiled, then nodded, his eyes still closed.

She tapped him on the nose and asked, "And did you

mean it?"

He opened his eyes, and she lost herself in that warm almost amber gaze. How had she never noticed the color of his eyes before? Something was so wonderfully warm and melting about them.

"Absolutely," he stated, a smile breaking free. "Never doubt that."

She stared at him. "We don't even know each other."

"Nope, we don't," he agreed. "The good news is that now we'll have some time to take care of that."

She felt tears in her eyes, as he pulled her down and gave her a gentle kiss on her battered nose.

"And I'll give you time to get used to it."

"Who said I needed time?" she asked.

"Me," he replied, with a chuckle. "I'm just letting you know."

"Just letting me know that you're staking a claim?" she asked in disbelief.

He thought about it and nodded. "Yeah, something like that."

"This isn't the Middle Ages anymore, so you don't get to do stuff like that."

He thought about it, then shrugged. "As I told you, I'm a dinosaur."

"And it doesn't bother you?"

"No, does it bother you?"

She frowned.

He chuckled. "See? You're not even sure what to think."

"Because I'm not sure what to think," she declared. "Can't say it's anything I expected to hear from you today."

"I'm not surprised," he murmured. "But are you telling me some part of you doesn't want to know if something is worth pursuing here?" She flushed and he nodded. "I just prefer to speak my mind right up front."

"Okay, … you're right. Something is between us."

"There is absolutely," he agreed, "and it would be nice if we had an opportunity to figure out what that was."

She smiled as she looked down on him. "It's been a while."

"A while what?"

"A while since I had a solid relationship," she clarified. "Both my brother and I just gave up on them, after we had a bunch of duds."

"Duds," he repeated, and then he laughed. "I've never been a dud in my life, so I'm not planning on starting now."

"I didn't mean you would be a dud," she said in protest.

But he laughed, then pulled her back down on the bed and murmured, "Nope, and I wouldn't be. However, on the other hand, I won't push it either. You've been through an awful lot of emotional traumas, and you'll need some time to sort through it all."

"You keep pointing that out," she noted in exasperation. "It is starting to get irritating."

He asked, "What part is getting irritating?"

"The mention of the emotional traumas," she replied. "I'm not wounded. I'm not devastated by any of this. Obviously now I have the absolute best reasons in the world to smile," she pointed out, "but even before that I was not somebody you needed to treat with kid gloves."

"Ouch, I didn't mean it that way."

"Good," she snapped. Then she laughed. "Listen to us. We already sound like an old married couple."

He opened his eyes and smiled. "A lot to be said for that."

"There is, indeed," she murmured, "but neither of us is in great shape to start a relationship right this moment."

"I'm in great shape. I just needed sleep." And he waggled his eyebrows at her. "You're the one who doesn't want to be treated like you're some lame duck."

She winced. "This is a stupid conversation."

"Agreed, so how about we stop the whole conversation and do something else instead?" Slowly and carefully, waiting for a reaction from her, he pulled her down until she was lying half on his chest and half off.

She stared at him. She knew they were coming to this point, at least hoping they were. She just hadn't thought that they would reach it anytime soon. And yet why not? Why not now that they had a pathway open, allowing them to have a relationship? As she settled onto his chest, she whispered, "I guess that means I should be gentle, *huh*?"

His eyes widened, then he snorted. "Have you looked at your face lately?"

She winced and shook her head. "No."

"In that case, you don't have to be gentle for my sake," he stated. "I'm just worried about you. You do have broken bones in your face, remember?"

"I'm fine," she muttered. "Totally fine, until the painkillers wear off." Then she leaned over and kissed him. And this time she kissed him with a ferocity that surprised them both. When she lifted her head, her eyes glazed, she muttered, "Oh my God, I don't even know what that was."

"I don't know either," he admitted, his tone thick and raspy, "but I sure as hell want to find out." And he pulled her down and gave her another one.

CHAPTER 15

MASTERS GAVE ELIZABETH plenty of time to change her mind, but she wasn't having any of it. Not after that first taste. She wrapped her arms tightly around him and held him close.

"I don't want to hurt your face," he murmured.

She smiled at him. "I'm the one who kissed you. I don't think hurting my face was exactly on the top of my mind. Plus those painkillers are helping."

He chuckled. "Maybe so, but I don't want it to get any more painful than it already is."

She shrugged. "Too late." She shifted. "You are wearing a lot of clothes."

And he looked at the two of them and nodded. "We are both wearing too many clothes."

She got up, and, without any self-consciousness, pulled her T-shirt over her head and then kicked off her jeans and socks.

He smiled. "It is nice to see somebody comfortable in their own skin."

"I've always been comfortable in my skin. Not everybody appreciates it, but this is me." And a challenge filled her tone as she spoke.

He grinned. "If you don't think that is even more attractive, you have no idea how my mind works." He pulled her down and gave her a deeply passionate kiss.

She pulled back again and repeated, "You're still wearing too many clothes."

"I can take care of that." And he was up, and down to his boxers in seconds.

She stared at him, stunned. "I don't even know how you did that so fast," she muttered.

"Doesn't matter, just accept that I'll always be better at some things than you."

Such a smug tone filled his words that she burst out laughing. Then, kneeling on the bed, completely nude, she shook her head. "You're still wearing too many clothes."

He dropped his boxers to the floor, revealing the proud erection standing right in front of her.

"Wow, I wasn't expecting that much action already."

He laughed. "Guys like me, we're built for action."

"Yeah," she muttered, as she admired what was in front of her. She leaned over and kissed the tip, and he made a shocked gasp. "The thing is, are you also built for the long haul?" she asked.

He grinned broadly as he lay her on the bed. "I aim to please."

"I already sensed that, but making me wait is making me cold."

"Oh, I can never leave a lady waiting," he murmured. As he quickly covered her, she moaned at the heat that poured in and around her just from his body.

"Good God, you're like a furnace."

"I am a furnace, yes," he agreed, with a smile. "Can't say I ever thought that was a bad thing."

"No, it's not a bad thing," she muttered, "but dear God." She wiggled underneath him, and, when he sucked in his breath, she laughed. "Probably shouldn't do that right away, *huh*?"

"Not unless you want it to be over, like, right now."

"Not just now," she clarified. Then she looped her arms around his neck and whispered against his throat, "I think we should have a little bit of fun first." Her hand slid down his back and across his buttocks, where she slapped him.

He chuckled. "Glad to see you like to have a little fun."

"A little fun?" she repeated, staring at him. "Can't say I'm into any of the other stuff though."

"No, it should be consensual at all times," he agreed, as he dropped kisses across her cheeks and chin. Then he moved slowly down her throat and across her collarbone.

She twisted sinuously underneath him, absolutely loving the feel of his touch. His hands stroked her buttocks and thighs and all the way down to her toes, and then slowly crept up the underside of her calves. When he touched the back of her knees, she giggled.

He lifted his head and grinned. "And you're ticklish."

"And you're not?" she challenged. "I bet you are some-where."

He nodded and moved away from her tickly spot. "I absolutely am," he said, with a laugh. "And please don't."

"*Uh-huh*, you just wait."

He groaned. "And that's fine. Just remember that two can play that game."

"Maybe not today then," she noted, with a laugh, pulling him closer, until the two of them kissed, deeper and deeper, more heat rising, as long sighs of joy and peace moved between them.

He gently lowered his head, until they were forehead to forehead. "Something is so very peaceful, joyful, about this."

She nodded. "Caring," she added. "I think that's the word."

"Maybe, and let's hope that it moves from caring to loving."

She looked up at him with tears in her eyes and nodded. "Now that … would be lovely."

He kissed her and asked, "You ever been in love?"

"No, at least not the real thing. At times I thought I was, and then it would turn out to be something completely different."

"Been there, done that too," he shared. "How about we decide right off the bat that we will work on whatever this is and will find that spot of joy for both of us here."

She wrapped her arms around his neck and whispered, "That sounds perfect. Honestly what would be perfect at this moment is if you found your place inside me."

His eyes widened, and he nodded. "Yes, ma'am." And in one smooth move, he was suddenly seated deep inside her.

She arched beneath him, now his total possession. She shifted beneath him.

He whispered, "Are you all right?"

"I'm fine, but it's been a while, and you're rather—" She wiggled her hips underneath him, feeling his own control starting to slip, and she chuckled. "Rather large."

He pistoned his hips, once, twice. "Unfortunately I'm ready right now. I want you with me too. Next time will be slower, I promise. Maybe after a nap."

As he started to drive harder and faster and deeper, she hung on for the ride, not knowing if there would be anything for her out of this. Yet, as soon as that thought crossed her mind, her body responded in a way she hadn't expected. She arched up beneath him, grabbed his hips, and started to drive for her climax, crying out with her own joy as her world exploded around her. When he cried out moments later, she realized that somehow the two of them were in sync in ways that she hadn't even expected.

When he collapsed back down and pulled her into his arms, he whispered, "You okay?"

"Okay? As a matter of fact, I've never been better." He chuckled, as she slid up against him and dropped her head against his chest. "Now, how about that nap you promised me."

"Nap? I thought you promised me coffee. Coffee would be good too," he muttered. Just as he rolled over to give her a gentle kiss, he froze.

She looked up at him. "What's the matter?"

His expression morphed, and he whispered against her ear, "We have company."

MASTERS HAD HIS boxers and jeans on in seconds, as he slipped to the bedroom doorway. He looked back at Elizabeth, seeing her quickly getting dressed. He placed a finger against his lips and motioned toward the closet. She hesitated and then nodded. As she moved to the closet, he stepped out into the hallway and froze. If somebody was out there, he should hear something. He had heard something earlier; he just didn't know what. He kept moving toward the stairs, listening every few feet. When he heard nothing more, he knew better than to relax. It just meant some intruder was waiting, in a position to attack, hoping that Masters hadn't noticed the little bit of noise that had been made.

But Masters had noticed it, and he knew that whoever was here in the house was a danger and a problem that they would have to solve once and for all. No way could Masters afford to leave Elizabeth alone at any point in time, not if this was the shit that would happen. Yet he needed to leave her because he had to continue working his job. He didn't know whether their intruder was after him or after her, but neither was acceptable.

At the top of the stairs, he listened for anything, but it remained dead silent. Too silent. Swearing under his breath, he moved down the stairs, until he got to the edge of the living room. There he stopped once again and froze, waiting, looking for anything that would reveal whatever the intruder had decided to come for, during this time of night. Masters heard not a sound anywhere, but he knew better. He waited and waited, and finally a noise ever-so-slightly came off to the side. He smiled and moved closer.

Just as he was about to surprise his intruder, a buzz came. Masters froze and heard somebody swearing inside the kitchen, right behind the connecting door, as the intruder scrambled to turn off his phone. It was a rookie mistake, and yet, in this day and age, often one that was overlooked more than expected because communication also meant they had to have their phones on.

Masters stepped up tight against the door, listening.

"I'm here, yes. ... No, I think she's upstairs. I'm just going up there. ... Look, I can leave, if you want. ... Fine, fine. I'll bring her with me." And, with that, the intruder ended the call, and the guy headed to the stairs. Except Masters waited in anticipation for their intruder to come around the corner. Just as Masters readied to attack, the intruder must have sensed something because he froze. Under his breath he muttered, "Shit."

Masters waited and waited and waited.

The other man swore again, then stepped into the hallway.

And Masters was on him.

The intruder roared, "I knew you were here, you motherfucker."

And the fight was on, between fists and kicks, with boots from the intruder's side and bare feet on Masters's side. It should have been an uneven fight, but Masters was fighting for everything that he had suddenly found in his life, and no way in hell would he give that up easily. He took several direct blows to the jaw, returned with an undercut that slammed the intruder back against the wall, then pummeled him several times in the ribs.

Just as Masters had the advantage, the intruder suddenly knocked Masters's feet out from under him and down he went, the two of them now rolling on the floor.

When a loud *bang* and a hard groan followed, the intruder sagged against Masters's chest. He was out. Masters looked up to see Elizabeth standing above them. In her hand, of all things, was a cast iron frying pan. She quickly turned on the hall light, still holding the pan, just in case their intruder attacked again.

Masters smiled. "Sweetheart, I always knew you would be a bang-up cook."

She looked down at the unconscious man on her floor, then back at the frying pan in her hand and giggled.

Masters smiled even more. He rolled the intruder off him, got up, then, grabbing her in his arms, he held her close. "Thank you." She nodded, almost numb. When he saw the shock on her face, he swore. "It's okay. It's all right. It's over with."

She took several deep breaths and nodded. "It's just—I didn't know how to get a good shot in," she muttered, as she stared down again at the man on the floor. "Every time I tried to get a good swipe in, it might have hit you instead."

He winced at that thought. "Thank you for waiting until you had a proper opportunity," he murmured.

She grinned and muttered, "Yeah, you should be damn thankful. I'm new to this. So who is he?"

"I don't know." He walked over and stared down at the unconscious man on her floor. He looked back at her. "Do you recognize him?'

She shook her head. "No, I don't think so."

"He was supposed to bring you back with him."

She paled and he nodded. "So, this, at least this part of it, is about you."

"Jeez, unless it's really about my brother."

"And that's quite possible too," Masters agreed. "Let me get a team over here." He quickly phoned for backup, even as he kept an arm around her shoulders. He explained to Jasper what had just happened, making sure to note that Elizabeth had conked the gunman on the head. At the term *gunman*, she was in shock, and Masters pointed to the weapon at the far side of the room that Masters had kicked free. She started to shake, and, as soon as he got off the phone, he wrapped her up tightly and whispered, "You did great."

"I didn't do anything," she cried out. "Oh my God."

"I know. If you're not used to this warfare, it's quite a shock." She just trembled in his arms for a few minutes, and then he suggested, "Why don't you go make coffee? We'll have company soon."

She took several deep, bracing breaths, then nodded and headed into the kitchen. He, on the other hand, bent over the gunman, realized that he was just starting to come around, so he tapped him lightly to keep him out cold.

When she returned, she asked, "How come he's not awake? Do you think I hurt him badly?"

"I don't care if you hurt him or not," he declared. "He entered your house with a weapon."

She nodded. "But still."

"I understand. And the reason he's out cold is that he was starting to come around, so I knocked him out again."

She sighed in relief. "I guess we don't want to deal with him right now, do we?"

"We'll deal with him because we don't have a choice," he declared, "but I would just as soon have my team here."

Almost immediately they saw headlights coming toward them.

"You think that's Jasper?" she asked, walking over to the window.

He moved her back from the window and whispered, "Just in case, honey, let's not make that mistake twice."

She paled and nodded. "Fine."

It appeared to be Jasper. And when Masters's phone buzzed moments later, he read the text and walked to the door and let him in.

As soon as Jasper walked in, he smiled at Elizabeth, marched to the gunman, and squatted beside him for a look. "*Hmm*. Do either of you know him?"

Elizabeth shook her head.

"No, I sure don't," Masters replied cheerfully. "We've got all kinds of these assholes coming out of the woodwork."

Jasper looked back over at Elizabeth. "How are you doing?"

She gave him a wan smile, then shrugged. "I'm okay."

"She's doing better than okay," Masters announced proudly. "Turns out she's wicked with a frying pan."

She rolled her eyes at that. "That'll be the joke of the ages, won't it?"

"Hey, there are worse jokes," Masters murmured, with a grin.

"Right, that's true. … At least we survived the moment."

"Now the question is," Jasper asked, "why did they want you?"

"The only thing I can think of is that it's connected to my brother. Maybe they thought if they had me hostage, he would willingly go back."

"Would he?" Jasper asked.

"Absolutely he would," she declared. "Yet they didn't need me originally. They needed him. And now that we have him, they might want some leverage."

Jasper nodded, sharing a knowing glance with Masters. "But they won't get him, and they won't get you."

"I sure hope not," she muttered. "From the little bit I saw of these guys, they don't play nice."

"No, they're definitely a group who doesn't seem to care what turmoil they cause, but they're after something. Until we figure out what, we won't get to the bottom of this."

"Maybe not," she agreed, "but we also don't know if it's related to that friend of yours who got shot."

"Mason. He's my cousin-in-law," Jasper shared, turning to give her a small smile. "Tesla's my cousin but closer really, like a sister. So Mason's not just my brother-in-law but he's definitely close family."

"Lucky you," she replied. "Sounds like you've got good people for family."

"So do you," he noted.

She smiled. "If you're talking about my brother, you're right. He's the best."

"It seems that you've also got Masters here," Jasper noted, with a chuckle. "And that is never a bad thing."

Masters walked over, wrapped her up in his arms, and declared, "I feel like the lucky one in this case." She nestled in closer, and he just held her. Then he looked over at Jasper. "So, do we take him away or do you want to interrogate him here?"

He frowned, staring at their prisoner.

She nodded. "You do what you need to do," she added. "I can always go up to my room. I certainly don't want to hear it."

"No, I wouldn't expect you to," Jasper noted, with a smile. "On the other hand, this guy is quite likely involved with the assholes who kidnapped your brother, so maybe you do want to listen in."

She stared at him for a moment, eyed the guy on the floor, and asked, "Do you want me to go get some water? We could wake him up pretty fast."

Jasper laughed. "Let's get him securely tightened down someplace first." And, with that, Jasper and Masters secured him to a kitchen chair, before Masters snapped him awake with several slaps to the face.

When the gunman opened his eyes, he stared at the trio before him, looking from one to the other, and groaned. "Oh, hell no. This ain't right."

"No, it sure isn't," she snapped, beside him. "Nothing about this is right. The fact that you entered my home to kidnap me, to take me away, and to do all kinds of shit to me, like you did to my brother, is not only *not* right, it's seriously wrong." And, with that, she backhanded him with every ounce of effort she had.

His head swung from one side to the other with a snap. When he finally rolled his head back, he glared at her and stated, "That's your free one. When it comes to my turn, I won't be making that mistake. You'll feel a whole lot more than that."

Immediately Masters clipped him a hard one and shared, "You won't ever get a chance to touch her. That's my promise to you. I don't give a shit if you die right here, right now. It ain't nothing to me. You broke into her house, and you had a weapon, so every one of us here would just as cheerfully bury any evidence to the contrary than take you in."

The armed intruder glared at him. "No way. You wouldn't do that. See? I know your kind. You're all full of ethics and morals," he explained. "Now, if it was me, that's a whole different story. I would have popped every one of you instead of making the effort to try and keep you alive."

"Obviously you weren't in charge of my brother's care then. Otherwise he wouldn't be alive."

"You have that right. He wouldn't be alive if I'd had any say in the matter, and then we wouldn't have lost him either." He sneered. "Not that he'll be worth a shit for a good long time. We worked him over pretty hard."

CHAPTER 16

ELIZABETH WANTED TO get paybacks with more physical violence against this man, but she also knew it was likely the only language he understood. Yet it wouldn't change anything. She stepped back, looked at the other two, and said, "I need coffee."

As she headed to the kitchen, the prisoner laughed at her. "You ain't got the guts for this, do you?"

She didn't *want* to have the guts for it. She didn't want to be a person who ended up thinking this was the only way out of whatever nightmare they'd gotten themselves into. It wasn't her way. It would never be her way. But she understood that, for some people, it was different, and violence would always be their way.

Standing in the kitchen a few minutes later, she poured coffee for the three of them. She heard the men talking in the other room, but she had absolutely no way to know if it was a good talk or an ugly talk. She didn't trust the gunman, but not a whole lot he could do about it right now, and she was pretty sure that he wouldn't ever see daylight.

If his partners in crime knew that he'd been compromised, she highly suspected they might take him out, but it wouldn't be her job, or Masters either for that matter. She suspected he could kill quite easily, when provoked. Hell, after seeing that man here, in her home, and realizing what he'd done to her brother and what he was planning to do to her, she could kill him herself.

That had never been something she'd ever questioned. Murder was never something she would have dreamed she would ever consider. Yet it did help her to understand a lot of the world around her. When she realized just how messed up it was and how something like this could change things inside you, she saw very quickly how someone could turn from a peace-loving person into a protective mother lion. That was exactly how she felt just now.

As she sat here, staring out the window, Masters wrapped an arm around her and whispered, "Are you okay?"

She twisted to look up at him. "I am. I was just thinking about how quickly we can go from peaceful to violent in a heartbeat, especially when somebody close to us is endangered."

"Absolutely," he agreed. "That's how revenge happens, and sometimes it can be a hard thing to stop. People always have their reasons. They always have what they consider as their priorities. Either they'll make good on somebody else hurting somebody, or they're starting off something they'll finish. It doesn't matter how it starts. It always ends up in a bad place, and you just don't want to get caught up in it."

"And what about you? Do you ever get caught up in that bad place?"

He shook his head. "It is a job for me," he murmured. "I believe in justice, in right and wrong. I believe in the good guys winning. And the good guys need a little help sometimes," he murmured, holding her close, his warm breath drifting down her cheek. "Sometimes I think I make a difference."

She tilted her head back and smiled up at him. "I know you make a difference and not just sometimes," she declared. "And it takes people like you to handle the assholes out there. I just know it's not a job I could do."

"And you don't have to," he noted. "It's one of the reasons I do what I do—as long as it doesn't bother you that I do it."

She smiled and shook her head. "No, it doesn't bother me. This work has to be done by someone, and my brother has already paved the way for it," she pointed out, with a chuckle. "I'm more used to it than you might expect."

"Good, then you won't have a problem if I continue?"

"I would never ask you to do otherwise," she stated. "This is who you are, and I would never take that away from you."

He kissed her and nodded. "Our little victim out there, he's talking up quite a storm."

She asked, "Why?"

At that, Masters shrugged. "Sometimes they do that. Sometimes they hope we'll go easy on them."

"Only because he's expecting to get slaughtered by his own people," she pointed out. "That's what his team would do to him."

"I suspect it's what they will do anyway," he warned. "Guys like this, they understand that they can't be left alive because they simply know too much. So, while he knows something, and he's thinking that maybe what he knows is worth something, he's trying hard to sell that bill of goods."

"I don't trust anything he says," she muttered.

"And we're not fools, so we know perfectly well what he's doing."

She smiled, then nodded. "Good. I'm not sure I want anything more to do with him though."

"You can go up to your room," he suggested.

"I am."

"Somebody will take him to headquarters and then to lockup," he explained, "and he won't go to the regular lockup because we can't take the chance. We have one down by our offices."

"Interesting," she said. "I don't think my brother ever mentioned it."

"No, he probably didn't, but then there may not have been any need to either." He chuckled and added, "Unless it's something he thought you would benefit from knowing."

"Obviously I don't benefit from any of this," she muttered. "Will you go too?"

"I'm not sure. If so, I will leave somebody here."

She nodded. "It would be good if you could," she whispered. "I just … It's stupid. I don't want to be scared. I don't want to be afraid in my own home."

"And you don't have to be, but these are trying times. No matter what we might want or not want, this is a very difficult time. We obviously know that somebody was after you, so let's not give them a chance."

"You mean, *another* chance," she clarified, with a wry look in his direction.

"Not another chance, but, hey, at least we got some sleep."

"We got a bit more than sleep," she noted. "We got a few minutes to ourselves."

"And there will be more of those. I promise."

She looked up at him and nodded but wasn't sure she believed him. His job would always be the kind that took him away, and yet that was who he was, and she couldn't change that. She wouldn't change it because inherently it would be changing who he was too. And that she wouldn't do. She carried the coffee cups out to the other room to see the gunman sitting there, still glaring at everybody.

When he saw the coffee, his face lit up.

She glared at him. "Did you ever give my brother a cup of coffee?" When he winced, she continued. "You're probably the asshole who would throw it in his face, even knowing it could make his day a whole lot easier."

"A lot of things could have made his day a whole lot easier," he muttered, "but only if he hadn't gone in the wrong direction in the first place."

"There might be a cup of coffee for you if I thought you won't be an asshole and go after me again."

"It's not likely that I would get you," he sneered, "not with these guys around."

"Yeah, I know, but I also understand that you might be somebody who would try, and I just don't want to live with that right now," she admitted, as she sat down.

"Oh, so I don't get coffee. Like I give a shit."

"You probably don't give a shit about a whole lot."

"I gave a shit about watching your brother suffer."

She stiffened, then nodded, as she relaxed. "Sure you did. That's what guys like you do, right? You victimize people, and, when they're secure, and they are tied up and can't fight back or even defend themselves, you beat them up. It's the only way to make yourself feel like a big man because inside you're a piece of shit. Your own mama would never look you in your face, and your dad would have dumped you somewhere alongside the road."

"My dad did dump me alongside the road," he snapped,

glaring at her. "And don't you talk about my mama."

"Yeah? I wonder how your mama would feel about you now?" she asked, studying him.

"She would be just fine. She knows we've got to do what needs to be done, when life goes sour."

"Yeah? What did my brother ever do to you?"

"What he was doing would have put away a bunch of us. So, he had to be stopped."

She didn't say anything, just waited.

"You don't know, do you? Do you think that I just like to beat up people for kicks?"

"Yeah," she replied. "That's exactly what I think. It's not as if you've said anything different."

"I don't have to say nothing."

"Course not. I don't care. I don't even know if the authorities will be brought into this. The way these guys operate in the dark, chances are you'll just disappear. Anybody you want us to write a note to?" Then she frowned and shook her head. "We can't write a note either. So sorry, that's just not happening."

He glared at her and stiffened in his seat but didn't say anything.

She continued to sip her coffee, as the other two men talked.

"Your brother deserved it."

She stiffened, then relaxed again, knowing he was just out to get her goat. "Did he?" she asked, with a smile. "Interesting that we have such different views of it."

"He stuck his nose where he shouldn't have."

"A young man was wrongfully convicted and then died," she noted. "How much of that is sticking your nose in where it doesn't belong?"

He glared at her. "And now you know too much."

She studied him over the rim of her cup. "I don't know very much at all," she replied. "I know you're a piece of shit. I know that I will wake up in the morning, free and clear, and your life will be over, but what do you care? It's the creed you've lived by all your life, isn't it? And, when this is over, you don't care if you live or die. Nobody ever cared about you, so why should you care about them?"

He glared at her, and she nodded.

"I've seen that kind before. The world owes you because you didn't get that nice, warm little childhood. So, everybody out there, they owe you."

"Nobody owes me shit," he sneered. "You don't know me at all."

"Yeah, I do," she argued. "You're the guy who looks at someone like my brother, and he's just nothing to you. You don't see that he's worked hard to help a guy in trouble for nothing that he did, somebody being pushed into something he didn't do, charged with things that he had nothing to do with. And you don't care because my brother went in a direction that you didn't like, and you figured he should be taken out. It's just that simple. He's like this bug to be squashed, so let's squash him.

"Yet the interesting thing is that that you didn't squash him. It cost money, time, and effort to keep Nicholas hidden for four months, and you had a reason to do that. Time and effort aren't something you're good at. You want in, you want out, you want your money, then you want to go on to the next job," she pointed out, with a shrug. "I get that. So why keep my brother alive? It's not as if you cared. It's not as if you had second thoughts. It's not even as if you gave a shit about where he would eventually end up. You didn't care if his body got eaten by coyotes or anything else," she noted. "So why keep him? That's what I don't get."

The voices around her stilled ever-so-slightly, and the gunman stared at her. "You don't know nothing."

"Nope, and you're not telling me. I don't give a shit about the rest of this. I don't care about all these cases, cases my brother might have been involved in, nothing," she shared. "I care about my brother, I care about what you did to him and why, and it's the *keeping him alive* part that I don't get," she admitted. "There had to be a reason. I don't think you make an extended effort like that without a payout, so what's the payout?" she asked curiously, looking at him.

"Wouldn't you like to know?"

"Yeah, I would, but we'll get there in time through this investigation. Maybe you fell in love with Nicholas, didn't want to let him out of your life," she suggested thoughtfully.

He looked at her in horror.

She shrugged. "Sometimes guys are like that, right? They fall in love with somebody, but maybe in this case you didn't want to acknowledge that you're gay or whatever. So you beat the crap out of Nicholas because, every time you saw him, you saw love, and you realized how much you hated yourself for what you'd become." When he started sputtering, she just smiled and whispered, "That's okay. I can keep your secret."

He started screaming and roaring at her.

She smiled. "Now I think you protest too much."

He fell silent, glaring at her.

"So, you are gay then," she declared, with a mocking look at him. "You're a big guy. I'm sure the guys in jail will love you."

At that he shook his head. "I ain't going to no jail."

"You won't go free," she stated. "So what are your choices?"

He stared at her. "Maybe I will get free."

"No, that isn't happening. And your gravelly-voiced guy, he's already dead."

He sneered. "He deserved to die. He failed."

"So did you," she noted, eyeing him curiously. "I'm free, and you're not exactly taking me back to wherever you're supposed to go, are you? You failed. So what makes you think anybody will let you live?"

He stared at her and shook his head. "I've worked for them for a long time. This isn't like a one-off job. It *is* a one-off job though," he corrected himself. "It's just that they know that I'm good for it. Even if this job screws up, it won't matter none."

"*It won't matter none,*" she repeated, pressing the point. "Because you won't be here anymore. You'll be dead, by your own people's hands. It doesn't matter if you were good right before you messed up here. It won't work for them because they can't afford to have you screw this up, and that's what you just did. You were supposed to take me in, but instead I'm not anywhere close to being taken in. You're late. You're not where you are supposed to be right now. Not with me. Not without me. So your bosses will know that you're busy talking away to us. Now they'll have to wonder what you told us. As far as I'm concerned, you're not that stupid. So you know perfectly well how they'll look at this. They know that you're done, and I can't say I blame them."

"You don't even know what you're talking about," he protested. "They know who I am and what I'm good for."

"Sure. Until you were compromised," she added. "Then

all bets are off."

"But I haven't been compromised," he pointed out, with a bright smile.

"They don't know that."

He stopped, glaring.

She nodded. "See? They don't know you kept your mouth shut, and you can bet that we won't be telling them that. We'll be telling them about all the great things that you shared with us, how their gunman is gay, has a thing for the prisoners. We'll see how they feel afterward."

MASTERS DIDN'T KNOW where she was getting all this psychological stuff from, but she was doing a hell of a job working up their gunman. Masters wasn't even sure if the gay gunman would get through this without having a heart attack, now that she'd positioned it the way she had. Masters just watched and waited, and even Jasper waited to see what their captive would do.

The gunman looked over at Masters and snapped, "I want immunity."

Masters's eyebrows shot up. "I can't give you immunity." He looked over at Jasper. "I don't think you can give him immunity either."

Jasper laughed. "No, are you kidding? Not after what he did to one of our own team. He's done for. That's all there is to it. He's done."

The gunman started blubbering. "They'll kill me."

"Yeah, they probably will," Jasper agreed.

Masters looked over at Elizabeth, just sipping her coffee, a blank look on her face. Yet he saw a tiny smile playing around the corner of her lips, as their visitor decided that maybe he should take another tack.

"I could help you."

She snorted.

And, with that, he turned and glared at her. "I could."

"I doubt it," she replied. "We've already got pretty well all the information we need."

"Yeah, but you don't know anything about your brother," he sneered. "I could tell you."

"Yeah, but that would mean that I would have to believe you," she pointed out, "and nothing so far tells me that you're trustworthy enough to listen to. So, what do I care?"

"That's not true," he stated. "I have lots I can tell you, and there's lots that you can learn. They do want him back, but he didn't give them anything before. So I'm not sure that they're terribly worried about it. They are a little worried about you though."

She asked, "Why me? I don't have anything."

He nodded. "I told them that. I told them that I didn't think you were worth fussing about, but they were all about making sure their loose ends were tied up."

"So, think about that and your position," she noted. "If they want loose ends tied up, where does that leave you?"

He paled and then nodded. "Okay, so maybe I'm not in as secure a position as I thought I would be."

"Ya think?" she quipped.

He glared but turned to the men. "I could help with your investigation."

"You haven't told us anything helpful yet, so it's not as if we have anything to go on."

"They were looking for something at Nicholas's house, and he wouldn't tell them about it. The more they beat him up, the more he just shut up. They threatened him with hurting you, but, when they never followed through on any of their threats, I think he just didn't play that game."

"And did they say what they wanted?" Elizabeth asked.

"Now that he's gone, I think they've decided that maybe they should check you out anyway."

She shrugged. "It's not as if I know anything. And, if my brother wouldn't tell you, what makes you think I could?"

"Oh, you won't withstand their version of torture," he told her, with a sneer. "Women always think they can, until they start getting raped. At that point in time, they always give in." When she stared at him in hatred, he nodded. "Y'all think you are so tough, but you're not."

"I can't tell you what I don't know, you idiot. So is that what that one asshole, Jim, used to do?"

He shrugged. "He liked women but in an ugly way."

"He didn't like women. He was scared of women," she sneered. "Is that your problem too? You don't want anybody to know you're gay?"

At that, he lunged forward and fell over in his chair.

She laughed at him. "Do you think you'll get anywhere in your situation?"

He stared at her, as the men set him upright again. "You're pretty mouthy while I'm tied up. That's the trouble. The minute I get untied, you can bet that you'll pay for it."

"Maybe, and maybe you're the one who'll pay. I just might have to keep my trusty little frying pan around."

"Frying pan?" he asked, looking at her.

"Oh, didn't you know that you got dropped by a woman with a frying pan?" Masters asked, laughing beside him.

The intruder turned and glared at him.

She walked over, picked it up, and showed it to him.

He shook his head. "That ain't no weapon."

"Yet it served its purpose. And right about now there isn't anything I particularly want to hear from you. So, as far as I'm concerned, I'm going upstairs." She turned and looked back at the men. "Unless you guys have a problem with that."

"No, we don't have a problem with it at all, unless you want to ask a few more questions."

"Oh, I've got plenty of questions, but I doubt that he'll answer them," she stated, turning to look at him. "I would just as soon let his homophobic brothers have their fun with him. The guy who's dead, Jim? It's too bad because he probably would have raped you himself."

"No, he wouldn't," the intruder snapped. Then he stopped and winced. "Actually he might have, if anybody got me down that long. Something was seriously wrong with that guy."

"Ya think?" she quipped. "Yet you guys were totally okay to let him loose in this world."

"Better to have somebody like that on our side instead of against us," the intruder murmured. "Besides, your brother never did give up the information they wanted."

"And what did they want?"

"They knew he'd been collecting information on a certain case, and they wanted it."

"So they kept him for four months. Yet Nicholas held strong, *huh*?" Jasper asked.

"This was all supposed to happen a whole lot earlier."

"So, what changed?" he asked.

"Somebody got fired from a position, I believe," the intruder shared, with a laugh. "And they lost access to something they desperately needed."

At that, both Masters and Jasper straightened. "Access within the military?" Masters asked.

He nodded. "Somebody was in a position where they could get what they needed, and they were looking for information to delve into, for information on somebody, somebody who might have had a hand in a betrayal. And they wanted that information, and then they would make a move, but he got fired. He's now dead because he couldn't give them what they wanted. They lost it on him. I don't know if killing him was intentional or not, but he's dead. Then they were stuck finding somebody else, but they didn't dare let go of your brother. And until that became an issue, well, now they're basically back to square one."

"So," Elizabeth added, "they wanted the information, and they needed this other guy."

"Yeah, he had part of it, and your brother had part of it, and, with the two parts together, they could solve their problem."

"Does their problem have anything to do with a recent shooting on the airport at the base?" she asked.

He smiled. "You would love to know that, wouldn't you?"

"An interesting thought," she replied. "It's hard to imagine that there would be this much shit going down on the base and not have it all connected somehow."

He shrugged and yawned. "I would need a whole lot more assurances before talking about something like that."

"Really? Chances are you don't even know," she stated. She got up and walked over to look out the window, and just then came a loud *crack*. Masters threw himself around her and flung her to the ground, landing on his back, as he rolled her over to the side, along the wall, out of the line of fire.

Jasper had already gone out into the night, as she stared over at the man tied to the chair. "Oh my God," she cried out.

"Don't look," Masters told her.

She turned her head in order to avoid looking, but it was hard. A perfect little brown hole appeared right between the intruder's eyes, and he was already dead. She looked up at Masters and whispered, "That was his own people, wasn't it?"

He nodded. "Absolutely."

"Shit, will we ever be free of this?"

"We will," he stated, "no doubt about it. And this? … This just takes the investigation up to a whole new level, but we'll need to ship you out, until the case is settled and you're safe and sound."

She shook her head. "I'm staying right here. I'm staying right here with my brother." Masters glared at her, and she glared right back. Then she smiled and whispered, "I have all the more reason in the world to fight now, so I'm not giving up."

"It's not always about giving up," he pointed out, "but sometimes we have to leave it to fight another day."

"This wasn't about me," she stated. "Obviously this latest gunman was here to get something from me, but this shooting? This was all about him and about making sure that he couldn't talk, wasn't it?"

Masters nodded. "He failed. And they don't like failures."

"Shit," she muttered. "I can't imagine a world like this, where these guys are just so empty inside that this is the sum total of their world."

"Usually it's about money or power or both, but, in this case, it might just be about revenge," he suggested, as he looked back over at the dead man. "What is interesting is that, when he denied this being connected to Mason's shooting, he was nodding his head."

"I saw that, and that was weird. I think it was a message. Maybe a message to the guys outside or maybe he heard something because he was killed right afterward. Maybe it had everything to do with a silent yes for us."

"The bottom line is that this investigation is about to kick into high gear."

Wrapping her arms around him, and holding him tight, she whispered, "Thankfully my brother is out of that part of the investigation."

"And we'll keep guards on him," Masters said.

"So, get them to move in a bed for me, and I will stay there with him," she suggested. "And, when it's safe to come back here, we'll come back together."

He looked down at her, a frown on his face.

She shook her head. "Let's at least be sensible moving forward. I'm not leaving my brother. I lost out on months and months with him. I'll stay there with him at the hospital. You've already got Tesla with her husband, so put me and my brother right next door, and keep the guards on all four of us. I'll always be wary, always be protective, but you can bet that nobody's coming back after my brother. Not again," she declared, "not after what he's been through."

Masters smiled at her and tapped her on the chin. "You do get protective."

"You know it," she stated, with a smile in his direction. "And I wield a mighty and dangerous fry pan."

He burst out laughing and held her close.

She whispered as she looked up at him, her arms around his neck. "Besides, this way, if we want to, we can always sneak off to a hotel room. At least we found each other."

He kissed her and smiled. "That we did. Now we just have to stay safe."

"Not a problem," she agreed. "Maybe you have other people you can hire to help out, guys you trust."

"Jasper and I do have a couple. We're slowly bringing our friends over to work in the department here on base," he shared, with a laugh. "Not that everybody here is somebody we can't trust, but—"

"I know. The minute there's that lack of trust though, it's hard, isn't it?"

"It is," he murmured.

"Stay close, *huh*?"

He chuckled as he held her close and whispered, "Like Velcro."

"Sounds good to me," she murmured.

In the distance, they heard the emergency vehicles, and he sighed, now sitting her up with him. "And now the chaos begins."

"That's okay," she claimed, "because, in this storm, in the midst of it all, you're the calm in the center."

He smiled and looked down at her. "I can't believe we found each other, with all this happening."

"I know," she murmured, "yet somehow it feels that we were never apart."

"I agree with you there." He stood and turned, with her still in his arms, to face the next step in this craziness. "Here goes."

And, with that, the front door burst open, and several team members raced in.

Masters looked over at Jasper, saw the expression on his face, and Masters nodded. "We need somebody else."

"I know," Jasper confirmed. He faced Elizabeth and sighed. "I don't know quite what to do with you though."

"We've already got a solution for that," Masters replied, with a smile, "if you're okay with it." Then he quickly brought up her plan.

Jasper frowned, then shrugged. "We already have to protect the rest of them, so we might as well. Pack up a bag. Looks like you'll stay at the hospital for a few days."

She smiled and kissed Masters, then said, "I'll be right back."

"I'm coming with you." He looked back at Jasper and added, "We need to get some new men, at least two, I think."

Jasper nodded. "I'll take care of it."

"I do have suggestions."

"Don't worry. I already know who we should ask for."

"Who's that?" Masters asked.

"Gideon first."

"You got that right," Masters agreed, with a laugh. "Bring him in. At least then we'll know what we're dealing with." And, with that, he raced upstairs to get Elizabeth packed, so that they could get her to the hospital and safety, ready for whatever else would come.

When he walked into her bedroom, she threw her arms around him, caught him in a big kiss, and muttered, "I just had to do that."

He chuckled, holding her close. "Come on. Let's go get you settled."

"I am settled," she declared, "at least on the inside."

And, with her bag quickly packed, he led her downstairs and out into their very bright future.

This concludes Book 2 of Man Down: Masters.

Read about Gideon: Man Down, Book 3

Man Down:
Gideon
(Book #3)

There is no greater motive than bloodlust, DNA, and revenge mixed up in a cocktail of hatred ...

Gideon immediately returned to Coronado base at the call for help. After hearing the issues facing him, he dove right in, knowing that he could bury the pain of his past broken relationship the same as he always had. The fact that they'd lived here in this city years ago didn't make it harder. Yet, once he caught sight of Pearl, it made it almost impossible.

Pearl broke up their relationship years ago, only to realize almost immediately that she'd made a major mistake. She quickly returned to Coronado, only to find that Gideon had shipped out overseas. Now still working at the same place as before, Pearl sees him in the stairwell, and the shock hits her hard, both with hope and dread. When she returns home that evening to something completely unbelievable happening before her eyes, Gideon is the first person she turns to.

Gideon doesn't know how Pearl ends in the middle of his case, but she is, and she's not moving any time soon. Now if only he could trust that she would stay this time …

JASPER WATCHED AS Elizabeth and Masters walked out, holding hands. Jasper was happy for them; he was. Neither of them had had any expectation of finding a partner in this lifetime, but it seemed like sometimes things happened, even when it was least expected. Jasper was happy for his friend. As he sat here, contemplating whether Gideon was the next person to call or not, his phone rang. He smiled to see Gideon's name on the screen. "How did you know I was just gonna call you?"

"Because, when shit hits the fan, it's usually me who gets the call," he replied succinctly. "How bad do you need me? On the red eye or will tomorrow do?"

"How about yesterday?"

"Shit, I figured you would say that. You want to get me caught up?"

"I'll send you some details. Where are you flying in from?"

"Don't worry about it," he replied. "I promise I'll be ready, in working order, when I get there."

"You'll need to be. We just found our navy investigator, who we thought was dead and gone. Meanwhile he'd been held and tortured for the last four months."

"One of our own?" Gideon asked in a shocked tone.

"Yeah. One who had been here as part of the military's investigation team, yet was more or less written off."

"Crap. Will he make it?"

"He'll live, but it'll be a long, slow road to recovery."

"Jeez. I'm there. I'm there. That shit never goes down well in my world."

"No, it sure doesn't for us either," Jasper noted, "but we still have a few good people to find out what the hell's going on."

"Yeah, well, I'm worried about Mason."

"You and me both," Jasper said. "He's holding his own in the hospital, but we're getting jack shit for an investigation going."

"That's all right. I got that nailed."

"Yeah, you say that," Jasper replied, "and you're joking about it, but nobody here is joking. So keep that in mind when you get here. So far, we haven't found anything. No sign of the sniper, no sign of anything, and this other shit keeps happening."

"And you don't know that this other deal, that *whatever else is going on*, had nothing to do with it?"

"I suspect it did, but we're still turning over rocks, trying to get answers."

"That's good to hear," Gideon said. "You know me. I'm one of the best rock-turners in the business. I'll see you in the morning." And, with that, he hung up.

Find Book 3 here!

To find out more visit Dale Mayer's website.

https://geni.us/DMSMDGideon

Author's Note

Thank you for reading Masters: Man Down, Book 2! If you enjoyed the book, please take a moment and leave a short review.

Dear reader,

I love to hear from readers, and you can contact me at my website: www.dalemayer.com or at my Facebook author page. To be informed of new releases and special offers, sign up for my newsletter or follow me on BookBub. And if you are interested in joining Dale Mayer's Reader Group, here is the Facebook sign up page. http://geni.us/DaleMayerFBGroup

Cheers,
Dale Mayer

About the Author

Dale Mayer is a *USA Today* best-selling author, best known for her SEALs military romances, her Psychic Visions series, and her Lovely Lethal Garden cozy series. Her contemporary romances are raw and full of passion and emotion (Broken But ... Mending, Hathaway House series). Her thrillers will keep you guessing (Kate Morgan, By Death series), and her romantic comedies will keep you giggling (*It's a Dog's Life*, a stand-alone novella; and the Broken Protocols series, starring Charming Marvin, the cat).

Dale honors the stories that come to her—and some of them are crazy, break all the rules and cross multiple genres!

To go with her fiction, she also writes nonfiction in many different fields, with books available on résumé writing, companion gardening, and the US mortgage system. All her books are available in print and ebook format.

Connect with Dale Mayer Online

Dale's Website – www.dalemayer.com
Twitter – @DaleMayer
Facebook Page – geni.us/DaleMayerFBFanPage
Facebook Group – geni.us/DaleMayerFBGroup
BookBub – geni.us/DaleMayerBookbub
Instagram – geni.us/DaleMayerInstagram
Goodreads – geni.us/DaleMayerGoodreads
Newsletter – geni.us/DaleNews